Magical
The Case of the
Christmas Crime

Written By Brenda Elser & Kristin Loehrmann
Illustrated By Rose Mary Berlin

ISBN: 0988690462
ISBN-13: 978-0-9886904-6-2

www.blowingleafpublications.com

ACKNOWLEDGMENTS

From Brenda:

As usual, I'd like to acknowledge the many people who make this process not only possible but more fun! So here is to my witty and lovable co-author, our Jr. Editor Nick, my friend and 'backup' editor Karen and to our beautiful grand baby Lilu who inspires our imaginations.

And for my husband, Bill – You make my world revolve!

From Kristin:

This book is for "Mr. Mighty," Julian Lambert, whose long-awaited arrival will guarantee many nights of Magical storytelling. Welcome, child. You are loved.

Contents

1. Ho! Ho! Hold On!

Christmas was drawing near and the weather had turned crisp and cold. Snow had begun to fall softly in light flakes, and slowly the world had become the kind of winter wonderland every child wishes for.

Eva sat in the window seat of her bedroom with her forehead pressed to the cold glass. Her wild strawberry blond curls framed blue eyes and her cheeks were still rosy from playing outside all day. She'd covered her legs with her nightgown and her feet were tightly wound up in the hem to keep the cold from her toes. Even though it was time for bed, Eva was daydreaming about the fun she'd had that day, enjoying the fact that she had two weeks with no school! *"And Christmas is only two days away!"* she thought to herself with a shiver of pleasure.

The neighborhood looked so pretty with the moonlight sparkling off the fresh snow, and she surveyed her yard, planning the exciting conclusion of tomorrow's snow fight. She had just begun developing a scheme to get snow down the back of Robert's coat (he deserved it for dismantling her snowman and claiming it as his own snow fort!) when she noticed golden sparkles rising from her best friend's chimney across the street.

"Oh!" she gasped, as the dust hovered above the roof in shimmers, swirling in lazy golden circles, until it transformed into… Eva stared as her best friend, Lauren, hung suspended above her chimney for a moment then hopped down to the roof as if it were the most normal thing in the world to do!

"Lauren!" Eva cried, tipping off the window seat as she tried to untangle her feet. She landed on the floor with a thud and quickly scrambled back up, pressing her hands to the window and calling her friend's name again.

Eva knew an adventure when she saw one (golden sparkles were always a good clue), and she didn't want to miss a thing.

Of course there was no way Lauren could hear her from that distance. Even if she could, she seemed to be distracted by something, since she was intently watching the night sky. Dressed in her warmest parka, her matching purple hat and scarf, and the thick gloves she'd worn to sculpt snowballs that day, it looked as if Lauren planned to be outside for a while.

Eva strained to see what it was Lauren watched for. Off in the distance, another cloud of golden sparkles had begun to materialize. Was this what she was waiting for?

As it flew closer, Eva could just make out the shape. It was...it wasss... A reindeer?

Now, Eva was no stranger to, well... *strangeness*... especially Magical strangeness, but before she could utter another shout, the reindeer pounded through the sky, golden sparks flying from its hooves with every step, and landed gently on the roof next to her friend. Eva almost fell over again as she watched it kneel so Lauren could climb onto its back. Then, faster than you could say 'Ho! Ho! Hooooold on!' the reindeer jumped into the freezing night air and expertly circled several times just above her friend's rooftop.

On the next turn, Lauren saw Eva jumping up and down through her bedroom window, and waved to her with a big smile. She urged the reindeer to come closer, pointing toward Eva's house.

"Oh, she's coming to get me!" Eva hooted. She grabbed her coat and rushed back to the window, wedging the glass open. The reindeer was close enough that she could see herself reflected in his dark shining eyes, and his warm breath made a foggy circle on the window, but before Eva could even open it an inch, Lauren shouted, "Bye, Eva! I'm headed to the North Pole to work as an Elf and help Santa! I bet I get everything on my list this year! See you after Christmas!"

Eva stood up on her window seat and crowed at the top of her lungs, "Lauren! You did *not* just fly away on a reindeer without me!" After all, *she* was the senior Junior Detective, and *her* family had all sorts of secret, Magical connections – not Lauren's! "Lauren!" she howled and stomped her foot.

"Tisk tisk, Eva," a woman's voice sneered from behind her. "Jealousy is not one of your more attractive traits."

Eva wheeled around, coming face to face, almost *nose to nose*, with… Diva!

The vicious former Tooth Fairy who had stolen the neighborhood candy and who had later kidnapped Lauren so she could lure Eva and Robert back to her castle and steal *all* of their baby teeth! They always managed to outwit her, but clearly they had not stopped their evil nemesis, for here she stood in Eva's room, looking very smug.

Diva glowered at Eva, and slowly a grin spread on her heavily made-up face.

"What are you doing in my room?" Eva sputtered. "Didn't the Tooth Corporation take away your wings?" She peeked around Diva to make sure there were no wings folded down her back and found that Diva looked exactly as she did the last time Eva saw her in Leprechaun Land – her wings were gone and her white hair was pulled into a tall updo, she wore yet another white ball gown and had on a sparkly tiara as if she were a queen of some kind going to a fancy party.

Diva stopped smiling and leaned in, glaring into Eva's eyes. "I used a little of my family's Christmas Magic so we could have a little chit-chat. Mumsy would be quite angry if she found out, so I don't have much time. Now hush!" She rotated her finger and to Eva's surprise, her blankets flew off her bed and wrapped around her in a tight cocoon.

"Stop it! I'll call my mom!"

"Don't you think I know that? That's why I'm hurrying, my dear. Now listen closely. I've left a little something for you under your pillow. I think it's time you and your friends stopped by for another visit, because all *I* want for Christmas is your baby teeth!" With a flip of her fingers she tossed Eva back onto her bed. "Oh, and don't worry about Lauren getting all the Christmas presents. Mumsy and I have fixed it so that *no one* will be getting Christmas at *all* this year!" Eva's mouth dropped open and Diva snorted heartily until she heard a noise in the hall. "Gotta run! See you sooon," she sang, her fingers waggling a spooky goodbye.

Eva watched Diva fading… fading… until she had simply *disappeared*.

2. On the One Hand...

Eva *would* have tried to follow her but she was still tangled in her own traitorous sheets. "Mom! Mom!" she shouted, sitting up in her bed. She shook her head and snapped her eyes open.

She was still panting and struggling against the blankets wrapped around her like a burrito when her bedroom door opened, spilling light into the room and framing her mother in the doorway.

"Eva! What are you doing up?" Her mother frowned and turned on the light. "I don't care if it *is* vacation – it's late. And what's all the shouting about?"

Normally her mother was very good-natured about Eva's enthusiastic outbursts, but it was clear she'd been interrupted from the very important task of tree decorating, because tinsel hung in her hair and pine needles clung to her sweater.

"Mom! Oh, thank goodness! You will *not* believe what I just saw! Lauren was riding a reindeer! I saw her get picked up by one – on her *roof*!" Eva huffed. "She popped out of the chimney with golden sparkles – like Santa or something!"

Eva had managed to get three fingers out of the top of her covers and she now wiggled them by her chin. "Golden sparkles, Mom! *Then* she waited up there on the roof until the reindeer came and got her. It just kneeled down and let her climb right on. Then – get this! Then she told me she was going to Santa's Workshop to be an Elf!" Eva struggled some more with the covers until her mother came over to help her unwrap.

"How did you manage to get so tightly wrapped in these sheets, darling?"

Eva took a big breath once she was finally free

of her bedding and shouted, "Mom! Diva was *here*. She trapped me!" Her face was red from thrashing around.

Mrs. O'Hare grew serious. Her brow furrowed and she tapped her chin as she sat calmly on the edge of her daughter's bed. "Now dear, are you sure that this wasn't all just a dream?"

"She... she said she left me something... under my pillow." Eva turned and slowly slid a hand under her pillow case. Then she yanked it back, as if she'd been stuck by something sharp.

"What's the matter, sweet pea?"

With worried eyes, she reached in again and brought out her hand. In it was a piece of paper with familiar hand-writing.

"Ah... *Not* a dream, then..." Mrs. O'Hare sighed and gestured for Eva to open the note and read.

With a trembling voice, Eva began:

"Dear awful children,

I've taken the Christmas Magic. Aren't you impressed with my crime?

It's my turn to have the last laugh - and I'd say it's about time!

All of Christmas is doomed unless you do as I say!

I'll be waiting for you in the North, where you'll finally give me my pay.

Diva,

P.S. And by 'pay' I mean I expect you to hand over your baby teeth!"

"Mom! What if she has Lauren again? Should we call her mother? Or maybe I should just go check her roof."

Eva's mother made a show of thinking about these questions for a moment. "Well, darling," she said, "Even if Lauren did fly off on a reindeer, I don't think she's in any danger, do you? After all, flying reindeer are very special creatures. Perhaps you should wait until tomorrow to check on her. We wouldn't want to worry her mother over nothing. What do you think?"

Eva's expression told her mother that she didn't think this was a very good idea *at all*. Lauren might actually be off in some dazzling, snowy wonderland that Eva was missing at this very moment. It was just so unfair!

"But what about Diva taking the Christmas Magic? We need to get the Junior Detectives together, mom! Christmas isn't far away, and Diva's going to ruin everything!"

"How about I check on a few things and then we get the team together to compare the clues over breakfast in the morning?" She took the offending note from Eva and stood up.

Eva scowled, "I'm sure I can't wait until tomorrow. I won't be able to sleep even one second. Besides, what 'few things' do you need to check on? Can't I help?"

"These are 'things' that I don't need any help with," Mrs. O'Hare turned off the light and smiled into the dark. "Now hush. It's time to sleep."

"Hey, mom?" Eva's voice grew soft. "Why is Diva always after us?"

Mrs. O'Hare sighed and lingered in the doorway. "Well..." she appeared to be choosing her words carefully. "Maybe it has something to do with Christmas this time... It's the time of year for giving, and Diva never learned how to do that."

"I don't understand."

"It's a long story, dear. Not to be told tonight. Now get some rest."

But as the door softly shut Eva knew she wouldn't sleep. When she was sure she heard her mother's footsteps padding downstairs, she flung the covers off and lightly pounced out of bed. Quietly picking up the socks and legwarmers she'd strewn about the room, she put them on under her nightgown. There was no time to change. She found her shoes and heavy jacket and threw them on. Then she snuck over to her bedroom door and cracked it open.

She heard her mother downstairs. "Hello? Mrs. C? How *are* you? Yes, it sure is! I'm doing well, and you?" Eva opened the door wider and listened. "Well I hate to bother you at this time of year, but Eva just received a note from Diva and it said something about stolen Christmas Magic? Hmmm... You don't say... And it's *all* missing...?" At this, the conversation became muffled, as if her mother had ducked her head into the refrigerator looking for something with the phone still cradled into her shoulder (as she sometimes did).

Gingerly, Eva inched her way over to the stairwell, craning her head as far out as she could without being seen. *Gah! Why does my room have to be on the second floor?* She intended to get to the bottom of this Magical Mystery and she simply could not wait until morning! Eva tiptoed down a few of the stairs. What if Lauren had been taken again? She could be toothless by morning! And imagine the destruction Diva could do in Fairy Land with the wishes from Lauren's baby teeth! She had to know more so she snuck down the remaining stairs and held her breath to listen.

"*None* of the toy production machines are working?" she heard her mother say. "Oh, that's just dreadful! Yes, yes of course... Well, please have them come by right away. Yes, I *definitely* think the children can help..."

The front door was within sight. Eva debated whether to eavesdrop on more of her mother's phone call or make a dash for the front door. On the one hand her friend could be in real trouble and might need her help, but on the other hand her mother was on the phone with someone who sounded suspiciously like Mrs. Claus! As in *Mrs.* Santa Claus! But on the other hand, her mother might catch her sneaking out and she'd get in trouble. But on the other hand, from what she could gather, her Junior Detective skills were going to be required to solve this case. But on the other hand... Eva smacked her own forehead. That was too many hands. She just needed to make a decision.

"Eenie meenie miney mo..." she whispered, gathering up her courage. *"Should I stay or should I go..."* She slid along the wall to the front door, glancing back briefly to see if she had been caught. Her mother's back was toward the door as she stood cradling the phone between her ear and shoulder. She was writing in a notebook. Gah! The suspense was unnerving.

Eva eased the front door open and slipped out into the night, closing the door softly behind her. The cold air took her breath away and she hopped up and down impatiently, wishing she'd zipped her coat first.

Hurrying down her driveway toward Lauren's house, she paused a moment, considering whether she should take the time to cover her tracks, but quickly decided against it. From the looks of it, plenty more snow would fall by morning, covering her footsteps and leaving no evidence! Eva turned and made a break for her friend's house across the street.

In less than a minute, she was in Lauren's yard, looking in her friend's bedroom window. The lights were off, and Lauren's mother and father probably slept soundly, thinking their daughter was safe in bed.

Eva began to pry at the window's latch. She would simply call to her friend, and if she didn't respond then she'd have to investigate. Her mom would understand her need to sneak out of the house if Lauren is missing, Eva reasoned. Quietly she tried lifting the secured window until the sound of a branch breaking behind her made her freeze.

What if Lauren's mother had seen her and called the police? What if her own mother had heard her sneak out? Wait, what if there was a masked burglar behind her right now, waiting for his chance to get in too? She held her breath. Yes, that was definitely the sound of snow crunching behind her.

Someone was coming for her. Eva turned her head slowly to look... What horror could possibly be waiting to get her?

3. Chill Out

"Hey, Eva."

"Robert!" she whisper-shouted.

The smug look in his eyes told her that he knew he'd scared her. Robert, her solid partner in Junior Detective crime-solving and arch nemesis in snow fights, now stood behind her with his hands casually in his pockets. From the looks of him, he'd jumped out of bed as quickly as she had. His snow boots were pulled up over a pair of red super hero pajama pants, his orange coat was misbuttoned, and his dark brown hair was in a tussle – as usual. Eva made a mental note to make fun of his pajamas at a later time.

"What are you doing here?" she whispered accusingly.

Robert whispered back, "I might ask you the same thing!"

"Well, *I* am investigating a very suspicious natural fernomanah!" Eva replied, hoping her big words were impressive. "And in case you were wondering, I almost karate-chopped you. I could have hurt you really bad, you know."

"Well, *I* am investigating *you*!" He paused, then asked, "What's a fernomanah?"

"It's like a UFO or something," she informed him, pleased that she knew something he didn't. "And what do *you* mean you are investigating *me*?"

"I was looking out my window, planning tomorrow's epic snow battle, where I win *again*, and I saw you sneak out. Whatcha doin'?"

"I got another note from Diva!" she whispered dramatically. "She was in *my* room!"

"Wh... wha..." Robert couldn't even form a

sentence he was so surprised.

"I know! I came over to check on Lauren."

"Oh, no! Did the note say something about Lauren?"

As much as she was mad at Robert for scaring her silly, she also knew he was an equal partner in their Junior Detective team, and the look of concern he now wore over their friend's safety was touching.

"Relax! It didn't say anything about Lauren." His shoulders sagged in relief. "But it *did* say Diva's going to steal Christmas unless we give her our baby teeth!"

"Again with the baby teeth!" Robert cried, throwing his hands in the air. "So, now what? Why are we at Lauren's in practically the middle of the night?"

"She just flew away on a reindeer, that's why." Eva waited for Robert's next stunned gesture. Surely he would be amazed at this additional clue.

This time, he nodded. "Okay, here's the plan: We're going knock on the window. If Lauren doesn't answer we're going to search for any kind of clues or documents that will explain what happened. Then we are going to comp-is-cate them – that's detective speak for 'borrow them,'" he explained. "And *then* we'll determine our course of action."

"It's confiscate!" Eva stomped her foot in the snow. "And it doesn't mean 'borrow.' Robert, this is *my* plan. Besides, I got here first. And *I* got the note!"

"Oh, chill out," he grinned. "Get it? *Chill? Out?*" He gently tapped on Lauren's window, still snickering at his own joke. "'Cause it's cold outside and all?"

Eva curled her lip and rubbed her hands together. "I *got* it," she grumped.

It didn't take very long for their friend to push aside one of her curtains and give them a squinty, sleepy look before she reached to unlock her window.

"What are you two doing here? It's nine o'clock! I was sleeping." Lauren yawned at them as she rubbed one eye with her fist and tried to smooth the blond mess of hair out of her face.

"Lauren! Oh, thank goodness you're here!"

Robert hopped up and down and said in a loud whisper, "You will not believe what Eva just told me!"

"We came to make sure you were okay… Robert, stop interrupting. I didn't even tell you everything!" She glared at him before turning to Lauren and continuing, "I dreamed you flew off on a reindeer! And Diva is about to commit another crime! So I, uh, we came to get you."

Lauren interrupted their gibbering by holding up one finger, "Neither of you are making any sense. And you haven't even introduced me to your friend." She added, pointing behind them with a yawn.

Robert and Eva froze in place.

"Hello!" a little voice peeped from behind them.

Eva screamed in surprise and spun in a crazy circle, squeezing her eyes shut and assuming a shaky karate stance.

Great! Now she'd have to save them *all*.

4. Lovely LiLu

When Eva slowly opened one eye, she was surprised to see a lovely little girl smiling expectantly in the snow behind them. She had soft brown hair in two neat braids with little curls sneaking out around her temples. Each braid was tucked behind pointed ears and her heart-shaped face was the perfect canvas for her large brown eyes and glossy, long eyelashes.

Eva turned to look at Robert, who was bent nearly in half, laughing so hard his whole body shook. "Ooohooo," he howled quietly, wiping his eyes. "You should see your face. You're like 'I'm karate girl! Watchhaa!'"

She looked down at her hands, still in her go-to knife stance. "Unlike some people, I was

Case of the Christmas Crime

ready to defend us," she grumbled, shoving them into her pockets.

The small girl looked back and forth from the bent-in-half-boy, the karate-hands girl and the girl behind the window wearing a purple nightgown. "Uh, excuse me," she began. "I'm LiLu, and Mrs. O'Hare sent me to get the three of you right away."

"Holy cow!" Robert shouted, straightening up. "A talking doll!"

"No, no, I'm an Elf. Santa's Head Elf as a matter of fact." LiLu tried to smile but it didn't last. Clearly the little Elf was troubled about something.

"I'm sorry," Lauren whispered, cracking her window open further. "You'll have to excuse us. We've never seen a real Elf before. Did we upset you?"

"Not a bit," LiLu said reaching behind her back and pulling out a cup of hot cocoa. "I've met other human children, so I'm used to it." She nervously nibbled her lower lip and took a sip.

"Did you just pull a cup out of your back pocket?" Robert sputtered, jumping up and circling LiLu. "How did you do that?"

"It's an Elf thing... I always have a cup handy in emergencies. Do you want some?" She reached behind and pulled forth another cup, offering it to Robert. He staggered backward in surprise and fell over in the snow again, gaping at the Elf, for once speechless.

Eva's mouth hung open until she finally managed to sputter, "If you're an Elf that must mean... You're from... the *North Pole*?"

"Yes," the darling Elf nodded. "But we really need to get to your house right away."

Eva grew pale, "Do you think it's too late for me to sneak back in?"

"Oh yes, your mom's waiting for you. And just so you know, she heard you sneak out... Lauren, get dressed quickly. You must *all* come. After all, someone has to straighten out this situation, and everyone knows you're the best team for the job."

"Ev… Everyone?" Eva stammered, confused by this sudden change of events.

"Yes, and we really must hurry," LiLu said, swallowing the last of her hot cocoa and stowing the cup neatly behind her back again. "I assume you're done with that?" she pointed to the cup Robert still held, its contents staining the snow and dribbling from his boots.

"Dang," he muttered. "I didn't even get to drink any of it." He handed her the empty cup with a frown, and Lauren rushed to grab her warm clothes.

"Uh... how mad did my mom look when you saw her?" Eva asked after Lauren had joined them and they were all trudging back through the cold to Eva's house across the street. She stood, staring at the lights in the windows and swallowed nervously. "Was she doing the finger tapping on the counter thing? That's never a good sign."

"I'm sure you won't get a lecture tonight. After all, Santa's visiting and we're in a state of Christmas emergency!"

"Santa? Dang it! I picked the wrong hand! I should have stayed at my house!" Eva stomped her foot.

"This is no time to dawdle... Christmas could already be lost," LiLu warned. Lauren climbed out her window dressed for the cold and the children hurried towards Eva's front door.

5. Just Call Me Santa

They were all slightly out of breath when they entered Eva's living room.

"Do you think there's any way my mom will believe I was sleepwalking?" Eva whispered, stripping off her scarf and hat.

Robert nodded enthusiastically, but Lauren shook her head and gave her friend a sympathetic look. "Sounds like she knew you'd left the house *and* where you went. She sent LiLu to come get us all."

"Children? Is that you?" Eva winced at the sound of her mother's voice. "Please come into the kitchen. I have a friend here I'd like you to meet."

Robert and Lauren raced ahead while Eva

slowly shuffled in last. Her mom stood with a stern look on her face. "My dear," she said, watching Eva drag her feet. "Later we are going to have a long talk about your late night escape."

Eva hung her head lower.

"*However*, right now I would like you and Robert to meet Saint Nick... or Mr. Claus..." Eva's mother fumbled. "Kris, what is it they should call you?" She laughed and stepped aside to reveal the legendary Santa.

A plump man wearing a red suit had turned around from his inspection of the pantry. "I'm sorry, Kathleen," he chuckled. "Your cupboard called to me. I sensed the presence of cookies in here, and I was not disappointed." Robert, Eva and Lauren gasped and clasped their hands together with sheer joy.

"Is this real?" Eva whispered.

He was everything they had ever dreamed of. His beard and hair were long and white (and

speckled with cookie crumbs), his cheeks actually *were* rosy, and his blue eyes were filled with a sparkle that could have only been described as *Magic*. One look into them and they knew they were in the presence of the real, honest-to-goodness Santa Claus.

"I think I'm gonna faint," Robert whispered, staring at Santa with wide eyes.

"Hello Robert," Santa rumbled with the kind of chortle that could make even an ice cube feel warm on the inside. "Please, children, just call me Santa. And I hope you *don't* faint! I could use some help from such a famous detective team."

The children raced toward him and he held out his arms to catch all three of them in a big hug.

"I still like to do that myself," LiLu grinned, watching.

"Why are you here early, Santa?" Lauren asked, stepping back and looking into his eyes.

For once, Robert had nothing to say. He just nodded dreamily and gazed up at jolly old Saint Nick.

"He's here because Mrs. Claus and I agreed that the North Pole could use your help," Eva's mother interjected, brushing the crumbs from Santa's beard.

Santa smiled at her and whispered *thank you*. "Eva had an unexpected visit from Diva tonight and she left her usual note. Eva, dear, will you pass the note to Lauren and Robert so they can read it? This one mentioned a crime regarding Christmas Magic, so of course I called the North Pole."

"Of course," Robert said, still gazing at Santa.

LiLu nodded and her eyes grew dark with worry. "The Northern Lights Magic seems to have vanished, and it's interfering with gift production and causing all sorts of chaos. We were hoping you could help us."

Santa tisk, tisked and patted LiLu on the back before taking a seat at the kitchen table.

"Us? Help *you*?" Robert squeaked, looking up from the note Lauren had passed him.

"Yes, you. I volunteered your services because you've been so helpful in the past with other..." Eva's mother paused for a moment, "...*Magical* issues."

"Yes, children, but we haven't much time to remedy the problem," Santa nodded somberly. "Christmas is drawing closer by the minute. As a matter of fact, I have been here too long already. I only meant to drop LiLu off so she could help start you on your way. Kathleen, why don't you and LiLu explain our concerns to this Junior Detective team. I must be off now. My dear Mrs. Claus will be worried, and that just won't do." Santa turned with a chuckle and leaned down to look each of them in the eyes. He gently touched their chins and said, "Listen carefully, children: I've told Eva's mother the Magic must be restored by the stroke of midnight or all is lost. Knowing how much you have done to help Magic in other lands, I'm confident the three of you will be able to solve our problem before it's too late and Christmas is ruined."

The children gasped.

"LiLu will get you started on your journey," he said with a wink. They each nodded at him seriously.

He gave the children one last pat on the head before touching the side of his nose. The children backed away, watching as Santa's boots begin to glint with golden sparkles.

"Kathleen, thank you again for the call and the cookies, of course." His red velvet suit was now aglow with gold. "And *do* give my very best to your husband. Tell him it's been far too long since we've had a good visit." Now his beard began to shimmer.

"Absolutely," Mrs. O'Hare smiled and waved goodbye. "Maybe after the holidays."

The tip of his hat was now engulfed in gold, and then the sparkles blinked out. Santa was gone.

The children stood frozen, stunned at what

they'd just seen.

"Ahem..." Mrs. O'Hare cleared her throat. "Come sit at the table, children. I know this has all been very exciting, but I have some instructions for you."

LiLu nodded from her seat at the table and patted the chair next to her. Robert rushed over without hesitation, staring at LiLu with a dopey smile.

Eva grabbed Lauren's hand and they both promptly took a seat. Another Magical mystery to solve! And helping Santa during Christmas! She searched her pockets for her ever-present Junior Detective notebook.

"LiLu, please explain the dilemma while I pull a few things together. I believe Santa left you the book to help with their transportation?" She pointed to a very large, colorful book on the table. How odd they hadn't noticed it until just now!

LiLu nodded, reaching over her shoulder as if pulling arrows from a quiver, where she retrieved a small, disk-like electronic device. She flicked a switch and a 3-D image of the North Pole floated above the table in front of them. "The Northern Lights – also called Aurora Borealis – are produced at the North Pole. The mix of hope and excitement from children all over the world gathers together in the freezing winter sky to create a kind of Magic that can only show up as... well... lights. It builds and builds until it glows in amazing colors. Normally the Northern Lights help to power just about everything at the North Pole during peak production season." She reached up and touched the 3-D image of the northern lights, which caused the picture to change. The children now saw Elves happily drinking cocoa and manufacturing gifts. "This year, it vanished suddenly, and the Workshop is acting very strange." She changed the image again by touching the projection. Now they saw the Workshop infirmary full of Elves with bandages and casts. Lauren's eyes were wide and Eva scribbled notes furiously.

"Since the loss of the Northern Lights," she continued, "our toy machines have slowed to a crawl, our materials are breaking, and accidents are up by 600 percent. But most importantly, The *TimeBender* isn't working! And after all your father did to create that for us!" LiLu moaned turning to Eva.

"My... dad?"

"LiLu, dear," Mrs. O'Hare interrupted with a warning look that did not go unnoticed by Eva.

"Of course. As I was saying..." she continued, ignoring Eva's furious note scribbling. "Everyone is working on a fix, but even if all the toys could be produced by Christmas Eve, we have no way to deliver them in one night without the TimeBender." The projected image of broken toys piled in heaps at the end of conveyor belts flickered in front of them. "Please, we need you to track down the Magic of the Northern Lights and return it to the sky so we can run the TimeBender and the Workshop can resume normal production." LiLu paused and looked sadly at each of the children before adding in a whisper, "That'll be the only way to save Christmas."

At this, Lauren moaned and clasped her hands together shaking her head no... Mrs. O'Hare put her hand on Lauren's shoulder. "You know I normally don't like to interfere too much in these things," she said, "but I suspect you'll need a few extra items in your detective kits this time. Eva, look at this." Eva's pencil stopped its frenzied scratching and she looked at her mother's outstretched hand. "I want you to hold on to this compact mirror while you travel, okay sweetie? It'll come in handy, so don't lose it." Mrs. O'Hare pressed a small, elegant mirror into her daughter's palm. Eva examined the lid embossed with scrolls and stars. She nodded and looked up into her mother's serious eyes, wrapping it tightly into her hands.

Mrs. O'Hare smiled at the children. "Here are your adventure backpacks. I've packed them with a few items that might come in handy on this trip. Robert, in the front pocket of your pack you'll find stones on leather straps for each of you to hang around your necks. They have the ability to keep you warm, so make sure everyone has a stone on. Got it?"

She kissed each of the children on top of the head and walked them toward the mudroom. "At one time, I was given a piece of advice that I think could be very helpful on your journey. Listen, now."

She stood in the doorway and spoke very clearly:

"Breathe to life your imaginings, for you'll be lost without them.

The keys to step north are found within, though you may want to doubt them.

Talk with the Magic of the Season and it will show the way.

In the end, what you need is the opposite of what you do or say."

"Talk with the Magic? Opposite? I don't

understand *any* of that," Eva all but whined as she scrawled in her detective notebook. "And why can't you come with us this time? This is a *big deal*, Mom!"

"Eva, dear, if I were you I'd be more worried about the conversation we're going to have when you return," Mrs. O'Hare replied. Eva gave her mom a sheepish smile. "Now, LiLu's going to help you, and I'm going to finish trimming the tree."

"Yes!" LiLu said, "Everyone come over to the window – and hurry! Time's wasting!"

The children clamored over to begin their journey. Eva stuffed her notebook into her pocket and pulled her hat on roughly.

Robert reached out and stopped Eva. "Wait for it... Waaait fooor iiiit..."

"Robert, we have to go." Eva tried to shake his hand from her shoulder when she heard her mother from the other room.

"Eva?"

"Yeah, mom?" she squeaked, throwing Robert a sideways glance.

"You will need to finish before midnight, as Santa instructed. Come straight home afterward, young lady!"

"Awww drat," she muttered.

6. No Time to Waste

"Come on, you guys," Lauren said, adjusting her hat. "You heard Santa. There's no time to waste."

"Hey, did Santa come up with the phrase 'There's no time like the present?' You know? The present? As in *present*? What does that mean anyway..." Robert trailed off, pulling on his snow suit and coat.

LiLu had already opened the front pocket and she now held up three necklaces with stones for them to wear. She held them up for the children to see that each of the stones had a picture of a flame carved into the front.

"I don't understand how we're going to return some Magical lights to the sky before midnight," Eva said, putting on her own snow suit and necklace.

Robert grinned, hefting his backpack to his shoulders. "If your mom has anything to do with it, I'm sure we'll be home in plenty of time. I mean, how does she know all this stuff? And how did she get my backpack and snow suit here?"

"It's like she *knows* things before they happen," Eva said, touching the tiny mirror in her pocket. "She keeps telling me it runs in the family and I'll know more someday too..."

"Well, of *course* she knows things before they happen!" LiLu laughed. "After all, she is The Great Kathleen."

"You *know* about my mom in Leprechaun Land?" Eva turned to LiLu.

"Sure, I know about her in Leprechaun Land and I know what she did in Fairy Land. I even read about how your dad founded April Fool's Day in the Court of Fools... But I know most about your mom's heroics at the North

Pole, of course."

"My mom's been to all of those places? Wait, what?" Eva paled. "You said my *dad*. What was that about him inventing the TimeBender thingy?"

"Promise me you'll tell me *everything* after your mom explains," Robert whispered. "*Everything.*"

"There will be plenty of time for explanations later," LiLu said. "But for now, Christmas is at stake!" When she saw they all were wearing their necklaces, she continued. "It's time to go now. This book will be your transport to the North Pole."

LiLu opened the book to a picture of a lovely meadow in winter. It was a beautiful evening in the picture and they could see it was softly snowing. A path through the snow led to a forest in the distance. The image covered both pages when it was open, and LiLu placed the opened book on the edge of the mudroom's windowsill so that the open edges were pushed up against the glass panes.

"*This* is our transportation?" Robert looked unsure. "This is a book pushed up against a window."

"Remember the first sentence Mrs. O'Hare said we should remember?"

Eva pulled out her notebook and read, "Breathe to life your imaginings, for you'll be lost without them?"

"Yes! So will you help me breathe this thing to life?" LiLu motioned toward the window. The children jumped up to help, leaning in close to the glass and puffing until it was fogged with a hazy mist. "Okay, it's just the right size now," LiLu laughed. "You can stop blowing."

"Good," Robert said, looking a little green. "I'm pretty woozy from all that heavy breathing…"

"Now use your imaginations." LiLu reached forward to trace a large rectangle in the fogged-up window. Then she drew a circle for a door knob. As the children concentrated, the

fog gradually began to materialize into a real wooden door. "Great teamwork!" LiLu applauded. "Now, who's going to open the door?"

"I got this one!" Robert scrambled forward and turned the now-solid brass handle, opening the door to the exact same winter scene as the picture in the book. "Whooah," Robert laughed, flapping his arms up and down.

"It's the same meadow from the picture!" Eva shouted.

"Exactly! Here is where you'll begin the search for the missing Magic," LiLu said, shutting the book. "Remember: you must bring it back to the North Pole once you've found it."

"You're not coming with us?" Robert stopped bouncing and turned to face her.

"We're too close to Christmas, and with the Magic missing at the Pole, Santa really needs me there. Besides with your past experience, I have every confidence you'll be able to save Christmas."

"You're probably right," Robert nodded, scrambling through the open portal and out into the meadow. "See you at the North Pole!"

But Eva hesitated. "I'm not sure, LiLu... This is a big responsibility..."

Lauren hopped up to join Robert, who was already making snowballs in the meadow. "You're allowed to get nervous, Eva," she called back through the doorway. "Just hurry up!"

"You can do this, Eva," LiLu nodded. "Christmas depends on the three of you."

Eva fingered the stone on the strap around her neck. She glanced back at the mudroom, took one final deep breath, and gave LiLu a tight hug. "I guess so," she frowned and stepped through the door.

7. The Northern Lights

Eva shivered, expecting to feel the cold once she was on the other side. Instead, she was quite comfortable. The stone around her neck grew a bit heavier but it didn't matter since it was doing its job keeping her warm.

The children waved at LiLu one last time, and she gave them the thumbs up and shut the portal door.

"Which way should we go?" Robert asked, tossing a snowball up and down.

"Elementary, my dear Watson," Eva replied pointing to the path across the meadow that led into the forest.

"Eureka!" Robert said with a little hop and a march forward, hefting his backpack further up on his shoulders.

"Eureka?" Lauren shook her head and smiled as they started walking.

"Geronimo?" Robert tilted his head and looked back at them as he walked on. The girls grinned and rolled their eyes at Robert's usual silliness.

"Aneeewayyy... Do you think there are any clues from what we know about the Northern Lights?" Eva asked. A full moon lit their way with all the intensity of a searchlight, and snow crunched softly underfoot as the children walked.

"Do you remember learning about the Northern Lights from school?" Lauren pondered out loud.

"I remember our teacher saying that they're lights in Alaska's sky and that the Aurora was named after the Roman goddess of dawn," Robert said.

"Wow, look who was paying attention in science class," Eva snarked.

Lauren continued, undeterred. "Right! Scientists believe the light's caused by little electrical specks that come from the sun and rain down into the Earth's atmosphere. The weird thing is that normally we wouldn't see any of this, because Earth has a magnetic field that kind of knocks all those speckles away." Here she made karate chop motions.

Robert and Eva made exaggerated yawns to show Lauren how boring her lecture was.

"As I was *saying*," Lauren huffed impatiently, "School teaches us about our atmosphere and the ozone layer and all that, but, according to LiLu, the Northern Lights are produced by the Magic of winter joy… So which is true?"

"I don't believe it," Robert scowled, stopping to make another snowball.

"You don't believe LiLu? Or you don't believe school?" Lauren asked, turning to him with her hands on her hips.

"I don't believe that *school* hasn't shared any Magic information with us. I'm telling you guys, we need to start a petition when we get home." He fussed, throwing his snowball at a nearby tree.

The children marveled silently, each lost in thought. *Somehow* Diva had taken the Northern Lights, and none of them wanted to admit it, but they were afraid maybe this time the case might be too big for these Junior Detectives to solve.

"We still have a long way to go," Eva sighed, breaking the silence. "Look at how far away the trailhead still is…"

Robert looked up, shielding his eyes from the snow that had begun to fall again. "Eva's right," he sighed. "We better pick up the pace or we'll never get there."

With moonlight guiding their way, and Santa's warning to solve the problem by midnight or Christmas was doomed weighing heavy on their minds, the children trudged faster.

8. Walking In Circles

"I'm getting tired," Lauren panted as they continued to walk. "Can we stop for a minute?"

"Well, no wonder," Robert nodded, pointing ahead of them. "It feels like we've been walking for ages and I'm pretty sure we aren't any closer to that trail."

"This looks like the same spot we started…" Eva huffed looking around at the same gentle snowy landscape. "And look!" she said pointing behind them. "You can't see our foot prints."

"Do you think the snow's filling them in?" Lauren asked, taking a few steps and looking behind herself as she walked. The children watched her footsteps slowly disappear, becoming perfectly flat snow again.

"Hey!" Robert pointed at a nearby tree. "That's the snowball I threw at that tree!" They hurried to examine the smashed snow more closely and agreed that it was indeed the same.

"Are we walking in circles?" Lauren asked.

"We can't be," Eva replied with a shake of her head. "We can still see a straight line to that trail in the forest ahead." She pointed toward the trailhead. "It's so close. Why aren't we there yet?"

"Hmmm..." Robert said. "It's like a rainbow – every time you think you're getting close to the end, it's still farther away..."

"Can we sit and rest for a while?" Lauren grumbled. "We can think while I catch my breath."

"It must be Magic," Eva said as she and Lauren huddled together on a tree stump. Robert wandered away and began kicking a frozen puddle with the heel of his boot.

"What else did your mom say before we left?" he yelled back to them.

Eva pulled out her notebook and squinted, holding it up to the moon's light. "She said 'talk with the Magic of the Season and it will show the way.'"

"Well, we can see the way. It's that path, right?" Lauren said, throwing a rock toward the trail.

"What does that even mean?" Robert said. He stopped his attempts at cracking the ice and turned as if talking to someone invisible beside him. "Hellooo, Magic of the Season. I don't suppose you could show us how to get on the stupid path, could you?" He leaned forward and began shaking his invisible friend's hand when they all heard a voice.

"Well, hellooo smarty-pants. I don't suppose *you* could show *me* how to get on the path, could you?"

Robert whirled straight into the air with a squeaky scream. Lauren grabbed Eva's waist and peeked around her as Eva waved karate chops (with her eyes closed) to ward off the invisible intruder.

"You screamed like a little girl!" the voice cried, hooting and snorting as it laughed.

Robert scowled, "Who's there?" The insult was uncalled for, and he grew brave in his annoyance.

"Who's here!" the voice responded.

The children gathered closer to each other and crept toward where the voice was coming from. Maybe if it was broad daylight they wouldn't be so scared, but somehow everything seemed a bit spookier at night.

"That sounds exactly like Robert's voice," Lauren whispered.

"Not funny!" Robert shouted.

"Yes funny!" the Robert-voice shouted back, laughing.

"Where are you?" Robert called.

"Where you are!" the Robert-voice called back.

"Keep talking to it... uh... to yourself..." Eva whispered. "We have to find you. Uh, it..."

"Keep talking!" Robert shouted.

"Stop talking!" the Robert-voice shouted back.

"What do I do?" Robert whispered, looking panicked. "It's just saying the opposite of everything I say. I *can't stand* that!"

"Hey, I know!" Lauren brightened. "Sing!"

"Uh, what?" Now Robert looked aghast.

"Sing, Robert! Sing!"

"I don't know any songs," he fumbled.

"Oh, please!" Eva said, exasperated. "Sing Christmas Carols. Sing the alphabet. Sing cartoon theme songs. Just sing anything, Robert!"

"Uhhh..." his voice cracked as he began. "Her name was Lola... She was a showgirl..."

Lauren and Eva stifled giggles and Robert clamped his mouth shut. "What? My parents say it's a classic."

"No, no – keep going, Robert. You're doing great," Eva whispered.

He began again:

"Her name was Lola, she was a showgirl.

Yellow feathers in her hair and a dress so debonair."

Eva clapped her hands over her mouth and held in her howls while Robert glared at her and sang louder.

"She ate merengue and did a cha-cha.

And while she tried to be a star, her gas could almost start a car.

Across the crowded floor, she danced from eight till four!

She was young and she had a brother, but just who shot whoooo!"

Robert's voice bounced off trees and snow,

ringing out with a tone that hushed everything around them.

"Robert, that was amazing," Lauren whispered. Tears of laughter rolled down Eva's face as she watched Lauren's mouth hang open in awe.

"Thank you, Lauren," he snorted. "I'm glad *someone* appreciates fine music from the 1970s."

"Wait! Shhh!" Eva said, abruptly sitting up straighter. "Listen!"

From somewhere nearby, they could hear humming.

"That's the song you were just singing!" Lauren said.

"Hey, it is!"

"I wonder if the mystery voice knows the right lyrics," Eva said.

"My version is better," Robert grinned.

"Shush, you two."

The voice hummed and warbled softly as the children crept closer. The Robert-voice began to sing loudly from somewhere quite close to them. Then it grew quiet again. "Well, *this* is hopeless," Robert grumbled.

"Well, *this* is hopeful," the voice boomed from directly under them.

9. The Magic of the Season

The children leapt into the air as if they'd been electrically charged, and the voice began to cackle with great mirth. When she'd recovered sufficiently, Eva dropped to her knees and began brushing the snow away with her gloved hands. "Come on, you guys! Help me!"

Robert and Lauren kneeled down, moving the snow to discover it was the same frozen puddle Robert had been trying to crack with his boot. When the last of the flakes were brushed away, the puddle was very clear, and Robert realized he could see his reflection as if he was looking into a slightly foggy mirror.

Suddenly, his reflection said, "Boo!"

Robert fell and scrambled backward in the

snow while his reflection had another good laugh. "This is incredible!" he said, standing up and trying to look a bit braver than he felt.

"It's not a ghost, is it?" Lauren whispered squeezing Eva's hand. "I wasn't prepared for a ghost."

"I think it's… Well, maybe it's The Season," Eva said, prying her hand out of Lauren's. She stepped forward to lean over and there she found her own reflection.

"Hello," she said. Her reflection returned her gaze.

"Goodbye," it answered with a cheeky grin.

"Are you leaving?" Eva asked herself.

"You are staying," her image answered.

"Oh, this is going to get very confusing," Robert murmured and scratched his head. (Faintly the children heard Robert's voice say from the puddle, "I understand perfectly," and laugh again.)

"Be quiet!" Robert hollered at his own reflection

"You be quiet!" his reflection hollered back.

"Robert, stop!" Lauren said, grabbing his arm and pulling him away. "We don't have time for this. Eva ask... uhhh... yourself for help."

"Okay..." Eva leaned over and looked at herself again. "Do you think you could help us?"

"I'm a reflection. I don't think at all."

"How do you answer questions if you don't think?" Eva asked.

"Hey, why is your reflection actually having an intelligent conversation with you?" Robert interrupted. He poked his head in front of Eva's and asked, "Why won't you talk with me?"

Robert's reflection said, "I will talk with you."

"Okay, so which way is the path?"

The reflection laughed again, "Which way

isn't the path?"

Lauren had to grab Robert again before he started shouting. "Do you hear that? Why is he, er, *me* making fun of... uh, me?" Robert fumed and stomped his foot.

"Don't take this the wrong way, Robert, but this is a reflection. I think it's showing you your personality." Eva and Lauren giggled at Robert's sour expression.

"Well, anyway, we're wasting time here," he said with a dismissive wave. "Go on and have a lovely conversation with yourself."

Lauren patted Robert's shoulder, staying clear of seeing her own reflection, and he sat down in the snow with a "humph."

Eva returned to the puddle. "What will you tell me about this? 'Talk with The Magic of The Season and it will show the way.'"

"It means that I can help you find the path," she answered herself.

"Well! You've always had a good sense of

direction!" Eva said, continuing the conversation. "If we imagined the Northern Lights, perhaps that would get us there?" Eva's own brilliant suggestion made her immediately squeeze her eyes shut so hard she saw spots on the backs of her eyelids.

But the Northern Lights made her think about Christmas Magic, and Christmas Magic made her think of the North Pole, and the North Pole made her think of Santa's workshop. So instead she sat, imagining what the inside of the North Pole Workshop would look like. Of course, it would have a conveyor belt for presents and a large train on tracks to transport the Elves to other Workshop stations. It would be brightly colored with wrapping paper and candy. (Oh, yes! Lots of candy!) She could almost smell the hot cocoa the Elves would drink on their breaks, and hear the Christmas music playing in the background. As a matter of fact – was that wrapping paper she heard being folded?

Eva slowly opened one eye and peeked with a hopeful heart. There she saw…

...Herself. Peeking at herself in a puddle. Her reflection gave her another cheeky grin.

"Aw, drat!" she said, opening her other eye. She saw herself wink.

"You imagined Santa's Workshop didn't you?" her reflection whispered.

"No!" Eva said.

"Yes!"

"Okay, yes..." Eva said. "But more importantly – I didn't end up on the path *or* at the Workshop. So... What do you know about the path?"

"What do *you* know about the path?" her reflection said. But just as Eva was about to become as exasperated as Robert, the puddle continued. "You know the path is right in front of you. Just keep going straight toward it."

Eva sat for a while and looked deeply into her own eyes. Something the reflection said was just too simple to believe. After all, they'd been walking straight toward the path for a while now and they weren't any closer.

"Wait a minute," Eva said, turning to Robert and Lauren. She fished around for her notebook again and read these words:

Talk with the Magic of The Season and it will show the way.

In the end what you need is the opposite of what you do or say.

"Don't you get it?" she clapped her hands. Robert and Lauren looked confused. "Okay, watch this," she said, turning to the puddle. "Black."

"White," Eva's reflection replied.

"Left," Eva said, holding up her left hand.

"Right!" Her reflection clapped.

"Thanks," she said, returning her notebook to her pocket. "So, we'll go in the opposite direction of the path."

"What? That doesn't make any sense," Lauren

objected.

"Oh, of course! Duh!" Robert said. "Our reflections are the *opposite*. So if they tell us to follow the path then we should do the opposite of what they say! That makes sense because my reflection is a real turd and I'm quite charming."

"Or is it the opposite?" they heard the Robert-voice ask from below.

The children stood up and looked toward the path. Robert gave the trail a salute (and the puddle one last good stomp), then he turned on his heels to face the other direction, making his way due opposite. Lauren laughed and tagged along.

Eva took one last peek into the puddle before joining her friends. Her reflection gave her a conspiratorial smile and said, "You'll have this whole Northern Lights mystery solved in no time."

Eva smiled to herself, trotting to catch up with the others, for a moment forgetting that maybe those words of encouragement weren't meant to reassure her at all.

10. We Come In Peace

The children continued to walk away from the path for quite a while, looking back across the field occasionally to confirm they were still heading in the exact opposite direction of the trail head. They walked in this manner until the path behind them was barely visible. Once they were at the brink of the trail disappearing from their view altogether they found themselves at the edge of the meadow. Tall trees stood in front of them like guards protecting royalty.

"Well, this must be it," Robert said. "You go first."

"Uh uh. *You* go first!" Eva said.

"You sound like my reflection," Robert grimaced.

They both turned to look at Lauren, who was tying her shoe and catching her breath.

Lauren stood up and pushed her blonde hair out of her eyes, smiling as she looked at her wrist watch. "Either time stands still here or my watch has stopped!" She commented. Her smile faded as she looked up at her friends, "What? What did I miss?" she asked.

"We were thinking that maybe it would be best if you led the way," Eva said, looking at her feet.

"Me? Oh, no no no. I don't think so!" Lauren looked back and forth between her friends. "Why me?"

"Well, you're always the rational, calm one," Robert supplied. Eva nodded vigorously. "Unlike *some* of us…"

"Wait. What?" Eva stopped nodding.

"I said *us*," he defended himself.

"Yeah, but you meant me."

"Okay, okay, stop!" Lauren shouted. Her

voice bounced off the trees. "We're *all* going to go in as a *team*, and we're going to solve this case like we always do – as a *team*."

Robert and Eva looked sheepish. "You're right," Eva said, taking Lauren's arm. "Of course, you're right…"

Robert took Lauren's other arm and grumbled, "I wasn't afraid, if that's what you were thinking."

Arm in arm they stepped into the trees. Around them, the air was still and dark, as if the trees were shielding them from the cold winter night. The moon filtered softly through the canopy of pine needles, and as their eyes adjusted, they saw the forest was sparse and the branches were heavy with snowfall. Some even bent so low, it was as if they were giants reaching their massive white, hairy arms toward the ground. There was a certain hush that only snow creates – a kind of tranquil quiet that held the children in its spell.

They could see that the trail was directly in front of them now – a worn path in the underbrush made up of pine needles and matted twigs. Moss curled around its borders as if it had been landscaped with purpose. It stretched out in front of them until it disappeared further into the trees.

"I feel like I'm wearing ear plugs or something," Robert whispered.

Eva could only nod. It felt almost disrespectful to break the silence.

Lauren moved slowly – almost carefully – as if she was holding her breath, looking at their surroundings. Her eyes were so round, Eva started to giggle.

"I know. Pretty cool, huh?" Robert laughed too.

The children relaxed a bit at the sound of Robert's laughter and released their tight grip on one another's arms as they walked forward. "Well, where now?" Lauren asked.

"I have no idea," Robert answered. "But I'm kinda getting hungry. Is anyone else?" He stopped and took his pack off, muttering, "I wonder if your Mom gave us any snacks..."

"Of course she packed food. She's... well... *my* mom, after all," Eva said.

"Yep, sandwiches!" Robert announced holding them in the air. "And hey, look at this! She stuffed three cookie sheets into my pack!" He pulled them out. "Was she in a hurry cleaning or something? Sheesh! No wonder this was so heavy."

"If I know Eva's mom, she had her reasons. You should definitely leave them in there," Lauren said.

Eva appeared to be lost in thought as her friends tore into their sandwiches. While Robert and Lauren chatted lightly, she took tentative bites and continued to look around them as if taking mental pictures. Finally, she broke her reverie. "Diva's note said she had taken the Christmas Magic," she mused. "That means that somehow she's able to harness the Northern Lights. How could that be possible? I knew she had powers, but I didn't think she had *that* much power. Do you suppose she has a stash of baby teeth we didn't know about?"

Robert, who was in the middle of a long chain of seemingly unrelated questions (which Lauren was doing her best to tune out) turned to stare at her. "Eva, have you even heard a word I was saying?"

She looked at him as if she just noticed he was standing there. "I'm sorry, what?"

"I was just wondering the same thing you were. How did Diva steal the Christmas magic? Maybe the answer will help us steal it back!" Robert said as he took another big bite of sandwich and nodded his head.

Eva opened her mouth to reply, but before she could utter a single sound, the children heard a series of crashes that shook the ground like an earthquake.

"What was that?" Lauren yelped, dropping her sandwich and grabbing Eva's hand.

The loud crack of a tree being snapped in half caused the children to jerk their heads toward the terrifying sound. There, lumbering toward the children, boomed a nine foot tall, white-haired beast. Its beady eyes focused on them, his lip curled, displaying row after row of jagged teeth. The beast let out a low snarl and stopped, tilting its head to the side as if considering the intruders.

"I got this one," Robert said, stepping in front of the girls. He held up his hands and shouted, "We come in peace!"

The creature's matted fur rippled over its muscular body. His black eyes narrowed and his nostrils flared. He looked like he would charge them at any moment.

Robert spun around and spoke excitedly, "It's the Abominable Snowman! The actual Abominable Snowman!" He looked giddy. "I wonder if your mom packed a camera," he said sliding his pack off. But this action seemed to unfreeze the beast, which threw its head into the air and roared.

"RUN!" Eva yelled, sprinting away with Lauren hot on her heels. Robert threw his half-open pack over one shoulder and sprinted after them as the beast rumbled closer.

11. Zigs and Zags

What the children lacked in speed, they made up for in agility, for as the beast crashed toward them snapping limbs and throwing boulders, they were able to duck around stumps and scoot over fallen trees.

"Over there!" Robert shouted above the clatter of cookie sheets bouncing in his backpack. "It looks like there's more light over there! I think we're almost out of the forest!" Indeed, moonbeams seemed to reach toward them like a welcoming friend as the trees grew sparser.

"Then what?" Lauren puffed.

Robert threw the squashed sandwich he'd been clutching and saw the beast stop to sniff the air. "Then we're in the clear!"

"What do you mean 'in the clear'?" Eva panted.

"Everybody knows the Abominable Snowman lives in the woods! Duh! He's not just out in the *open* all day!"

Eva and Lauren would have cried in relief... if they didn't suspect that Robert was probably making up what he knew about Abominable Snowmen. But the beast spotted Robert's sandwich and slowed to investigate its contents, and they didn't waste a moment arguing about what "everybody" knew of woods and hairy predators.

Racing over the scrubby vegetation, they emerged on the other side of the forest and into the moonlight. Snow fell softly around them as they slowed to look at the nearby valley to find a hiding spot.

"Whoah," Robert gasped stopping suddenly. "What *is* that?" Off in the distance, snowflakes appeared to be electrically charged with color as if illuminated by a kaleidoscope of lights.

The children ducked behind a large, thorny bush, and peeked around it to gaze at the pops of color disappearing from the sky over the valley.

"Robert," Eva whispered in between breaths, "you keep watch for the A-bomb and Lauren and I are going to take a closer look."

Robert nodded and squinted back toward the forest. "I'll make a robot sound to warn you if I see him coming."

"What does that even mean?" Eva frowned. "Why a robot?"

"Because they're *cool*, that's why. Besides if I made a noise like an owl, how would you know it was me and not a real owl? Duh!"

"Actually, I'd be fine if we all stuck together," Lauren whispered, clutching her friends' hands. "Because I think we may have just found the Northern Lights."

Robert gazed into the distance. In the midnight blue of the sky, there appeared to be an outline of a large structure. "Do you guys see that? It looks like the building where my dad works."

"What could a building like that possibly be doing out here?" Eva wondered aloud.

"Hey!" Lauren sputtered. But before she could say another word, Robert and Eva saw it: The hovering cloud of ever-changing lights began flowing toward a dark, black hole.

"Oh my gosh, that's where the Northern Lights are disappearing! Come on – we better get going before they're all gone."

The children had just crept from behind the bush when the forest behind them began to rumble. The creature crashed through the trees and into the snowy clearing, howling his wrath and pounding straight toward them.

Robert shouted, "Beep, Beep, Boop-Bop!" and began jerking his arms and legs in stiff robot form.

"Yes, yes! We know!" Lauren shrieked, and they all broke into another sprint toward the smoothly sloping valley, ducking boulders and dodging snowballs that seemed to fly within inches of them.

"Ouch! Hey!" Robert shouted, as crystals from a snowball cut through one of the straps of his backpack. "He throws *hard*!"

Lauren sobbed, "At least you have cookie sheets for a shield!"

"Wait a minute!" Eva panted. "Cookie sheets!" Robert and Lauren strained to hear her over the rumbling ground and roaring displeasure of the monster not far behind. There were no trees to shelter them, and agility was no longer in their favor. They needed *speed*. "Cookie sheets! And a paper bag! Hurry!"

"Have you lost your mind?" Robert panted back. Though they were all wearing warmth stones, it did nothing for the frigid night air they gasped into their lungs as they ran, and he could barely finish the snarky question.

"Snowboard!" Eva yelled.

"Ahhh!" Robert nodded with glee. "Best...

idea... ever..." He reached clumsily into his half-open pack and yanked the zipper. The cookie sheets clanked to the ground and the children lurched to scoop them up without breaking stride.

Another snowball shot over their heads and bounced down the hill picking up speed. The Snowman roared again in fury. "He's catching up!" Lauren cried.

If he doesn't catch us, he'll take us out with a deadly canon ball of snow! Eva thought. Instead, she shouted, "Toward the building! Go!" Robert hopped onto his cookie sheet and shoved off. "Wait! Robert, we have to stick together!"

But it was too late. Robert careened down the slope and Eva's words were drowned out by another howl. Grabbing tightly to each other's hands, Lauren and Eva stepped onto their cookie sheets. "It's now or never!" Eva said as the Snowman stomped toward them.

"Now!" Lauren squealed in fright

The girls launched down the hill, unsteadily avoiding dips and swerving around bumps. By comparison, Robert looked as graceful as a professional snowboarder, while Lauren could barely see through her tears – but it was working! They were putting more and more distance between themselves and the dreadful monster, which could not keep track of all their zigs and zags and was so far behind they could not see him any longer.

"We're almost there, Lauren! Just keep holding my hand!"

Lauren snuck a grin at her friend, but kept her eyes on the snow. They were losing the beast (who was a tiny dot off in the distance now) and they'd almost caught up to Robert! He was just downslope from them! Just another few feet and...

"Aheeeee..." Suddenly the girls heard Robert's cries as he dropped from view.

"Robert!" Eva cried, coming to a spinning stop right at the edge of the embankment her friend had just careened over. "Robert!"

"Is he there?" Lauren asked. She had skidded to a stop beside Eva by sitting down and dragging her hands in the snow.

"I'm okay," Robert called up. "I'm near a ledge."

"Okay, hold on. I'm pretty sure we can get to you. We'll come down there and pull you to where the ledge gets wider."

"*Pretty* sure you can get to me?" Robert called back up to them. He was laying on his stomach trying to brace his feet against something – anything – but it was no use. He was sliding backward... "Oh my gosh! Oh my gosh!" he squealed until his foot hit something and his descent down the ridge stopped.

The girls climbed as quickly as they could down to the ledge where Robert's body rested precariously.

"I don't think the beast will find us down here," Eva assured her friends.

Robert held his breath and slooowly spread

his arms and legs out until he was laying spread eagle. He looked like he was making an upside-down snow angel. He didn't dare to raise his head as he extended his hand to Eva.

"Robert, the ledge is thinner where you are. I'm going to stretch out and grab your hand. Just hold still! Don't move!"

"Ooo... Ohh... Okay..." Robert whispered. He was afraid that even his breath might cause him to slide again, so he was definitely not planning on moving even a muscle.

"Robert, I can't quite get to you." Eva grunted. "Lauren, hold my hand so we can make a chain and then I'll stretch as far as I can to reach him. Don't let go! Anyone!"

Robert flattened himself on the ground, searching for another rock or sturdy root to brace his feet against, but found nothing solid. Lauren quickly gripped Eva's hand and nodded that she was ready.

Eva stretched out, one hand holding Lauren's

and the other reaching as far as she could until finally she grasped Robert's hand. "I've got you, Robert. Hold on!" Slowly Lauren and Eva pulled Robert toward them until he was back on the wide, solid part of the ledge. Robert looked up and saw that the ledge formed a lip and they were in a shallow cave of sorts. "I almost fell," he trembled. "I was THIS close." He shuddered, holding up his fingers to show the inch of space he had before his fall.

"Oh, thank goodness you didn't fall into that ravine!" Lauren cried, hugging her shivering friend.

Robert opened his mouth to thank his friends, but he was so afraid he'd cry (and get teased by Eva) that all he could do was pull the girls into a hug and laugh in the way only a person who has narrowly escaped an untimely demise can laugh.

Their celebration did not last long. The screams of the beast came from overhead now, causing a swift jolt in the children's relief. Instinctively they flattened their backs against the hard dirt wall, terrified they'd be spotted.

When it became silent again, Robert whispered, "Okay, I think he's gone."

"No, I hear heavy breathing," Lauren looked doubtful. The snow muffled every sound, while the children listened intently.

"One of us should look."

With a sigh, Robert crawled the short way back so he could poke his head up over the drop-off. There, he found himself face to face with the drooling, panting, Abominable Snowman. Its eyes burned red and its flat nostrils flared, blowing puffs of steam into the frigid air.

"Uhhh..." Robert's voice shook. From the sound of it, Eva knew they'd been discovered. "Hello there. How was the sandwich?"

The beast reached for him but Robert twisted away and slipped back down the embankment until Lauren caught the quaking boy before he could slip any farther.

"It's Go Time!" Eva shouted, reaching for the paper lunch bag in her pocket. "He's right where we want him! Time to blow up those bags!"

The children grabbed their bags and began blowing into them until the sacks had expanded into smallish paper balloons. The Snowman's long arm swiped at them as he leaned over the ravine and he grew more and more agitated since they were just out of his reach. Lauren stopped to catch her breath, but when the hairs from his reaching arm grazed her, she screamed so loud it reverberated through the canyon.

Then silence.

As the echoes died down, the children could hear only their own panting breaths. "Is he gone?" Lauren trembled. They sat in the quiet, straining to hear any sound of the beast's snorting growls.

Then a low rumble shook the ground. "On the

count of three we pop the bags!" Eva shouted. The terrified friends held their bags at the ready.

Just then, the beast's claws snagged the hood of Robert's jacket and he shrieked, "Maybe on the count of one!"

"ONE!" Eva yelled. The children slapped their paper bags, and as they exploded, the field echoed with a loud crack that caused the Snowman to drop Robert and turn to look around.

He lifted his nose to the air, cocking his head to listen. The boom sounded like it was coming from all directions, rumbling off the snow, out of the canyon, off the ledge. The creature whirled in circles, determined to hunt it down and stop it.

The children backed up and braced themselves against the wall of the shallow cavern as the rumble grew louder. Lauren shut his eyes and cried, "He's going to eat us! Listen to his stomach!"

"I don't think that's his stomach!" Eva shouted as the monster dropped to all fours and grabbed for the sobbing Lauren.

As he leaned further out on the rim to reach the children below, a rolling wave of snow dislodged and picked up the beast, hurtling him down, past the children's safe little cave and into the gully far below. Crashing down through the trees and boulders, the creature roared and howled, until the children could no longer hear him and the meadow was once again silent.

The clever Junior Detective team held their breath, still pressed against the rock, until they were sure it was safe. "My plan worked," Eva said. "I think…" Crawling to the edge of the cliff, they peeked over the side to see that the Snowman had reached the very bottom and was trying to dig his way out.

"Well," Robert said, "that should take him awhile."

"I'm not ready to take any chances," Lauren said, wiping his eyes. "Let's get out of here."

Eva and Robert nodded and looked toward the evening sky. How much time did they have before midnight? While time *did* seem different in Magical lands...they may have missed their chance to save Christmas.

12. A Fierce, Winged Beast!

After a lot of unsteady hiking, the children had finally worked their way down the opposite side of rocky cliff. The hillside was dotted with trees, and many had not fared well in the avalanche. Icy limbs had snapped under the extra weight, making their escape difficult to navigate. No one wanted to experience the same fate as the Snowman so their measured steps were planted cautiously, putting more and more distance between themselves and the beast.

"Just keep moving toward those lights," Eva directed, looking at her wrist. "Hey, my watch must have stopped too."

"Well my *stomach* watch didn't stop," Robert complained. "I wish I hadn't given that

Abominable Snow Rug my sandwich. I'm really hungry. Do you think your mom packed anything else?" He began to dig in his pack when he ran right into the girls, who had frozen in their tracks and were gripping each other's hands in fear.

"Hey!" Robert growled, dropping to his knees to retrieve the contents of his spilled backpack. "A little warning next time?" But his next irritated comment was cut short when he looked up and saw the source of their dismay.

Just down the hill through the trees, a massive building rose up from the snow. Now that they were closer, they saw the Northern Lights weren't *passively* flowing toward a dark black hole like Eva had said. They were being sucked into the ravenous mouth of an enormous dragon!

"The guys at school are never going to believe this!" Robert stood up, gasping as he watched the flying dragon inhale the colorful lights like a giant vacuum.

"Robert, lower your voice," Eva admonished. But it was too late. In the quiet snowfall, Robert's voice had travelled, seemingly cutting a straight path from his mouth to the dragon's ears.

The startled creature cocked his head like some kind of fantastic winged puppy and locked eyes with Robert. "Uh, guys?" Robert's voice was low. "It's looking straight at us."

The dragon hovered above the building, its wings fanning the air gracefully, its tail swishing back and forth like a wary cat. Inside its distended belly, the children could see the shimmering reds and greens of the Aurora Borealis giving the effect of some kind of cosmic nightlight.

"Great," Eva said. "First the Abominable Snowman, now a glowing dragon."

"What now?" Lauren's voice trembled again.

"Well, I'm fresh out of sandwiches, so that's not an option."

But before they could come up with another

plan, they saw the dragon droop and yawn. It rubbed its swollen belly and let out a small burp, causing a puff of shimmering blue light to escape from its nostrils and float back into the sky. The dragon turned from them, looking off into the distance, and dove, swooping and diving, until it was out of sight.

"Where'd he go?" Lauren squinted.

"Look, you guys," Eva pointed as she caught a glimpse of its landing. "I can just see the tip of his tail over the edge of the building." Indeed, the dragon had landed on the roof and appeared to be lying down like a lizard lays on a rock warmed in the sun.

"And look – no more lights." Lauren pointed at the now dark sky.

They scanned the sky for any traces of red or green, but all that remained was a faint glow on the roof of the building the dragon had landed on.

"Looks like the *dragon* is our culprit, not Diva!" Robert said. "We better get down there."

The children tightened their backpacks and began walking. The snow was firm under their feet and the full moon lit the way. "How do we get the lights out of a dragon's belly?" Lauren wondered as she lagged behind her friends.

But Eva and Robert had already trotted ahead, out of earshot, ready to take on the fierce winged beast.

13. We Are Family

When the three of them stood in front of the building's entrance, Eva read the sign over the door, "'Snow Corporation, LLC. We Make The World A Whiter Winter Place.' Hmmm…"

"What *is* this place?" Lauren said, scanning the 20-foot high transparent ice doors that opened to a marble tiled lobby. Now that they were closer, they could see the building, which had looked like concrete and glass from farther away, was made entirely of stone and ice.

"I'm not sure, but we saw the dragon with the lights in its belly is on *this* roof, so we have to go in." Eva said turning to her friends.

Robert hesitated uncharacteristically, "I don't know… If this place is anything like my Dad's office, everyone is really fussy. And they pinch your cheeks. And they're always asking you what you want to be when you grow up. Can't we just sneak in?"

"Oh, Robert!" Lauren rolled her eyes "That's just a grownup's way of being nice. Besides, there couldn't possibly be anyone here at this time."

"Fine," he nodded, looking unsure. "For *Christmas*... Let's do this."

Eva pushed the door and it swung open easily. The children entered the lobby and looked around. Ice sculptures adorned the carved archways, and fluffy snow couches flanked a solid ice table filled with magazines.

"Does this place remind you of anything?" Robert asked.

"There *is* a lot of white... You don't think... This couldn't possibly be..." Eva stammered.

The three fell silent. No one would say what they were all thinking: This building bore an uncanny resemblance to the homes of their former Tooth Fairy, Diva. The children trembled remembering the evil Fairy who had stolen the Halloween Candy from their entire town; who had imprisoned them in her Decaying Dungeons waiting for their baby teeth to fall out so she could harness its Magical wish power; who had launched her ear wax guards after them in Leprechaun Land when they were trying to rescue Lauren. Surely, in yet another Magical land, this wicked creature couldn't possibly have set up business! Could she?

"Excuse me, may I help you?" they heard someone ask from across the room.

"Yikes!" Lauren jumped. "Who said that?"

"Over here," said the voice. "At the welcome desk."

The children saw that, indeed, there was a very petite woman sitting at a very large reception counter. She had lovely pale skin and wore a tailored ice blue suit. She would have looked like any typical receptionist except for the fire stone she wore around her neck.

"You're not a dragon," Robert said flatly.

The woman chuckled. "No. I'm the receptionist."

"A warmth stone," Eva said pointing at her necklace.

"That's right," she nodded. "Is that what you're looking for? Because we don't sell them here."

"No, uh… No…we, uh…" Eva sputtered looking at her friends. "Wow, you're open late."

"Round the clock!" she chirped.

"Is it possible to speak to the person in charge?" Lauren intervened.

"You're here to see Ms. Crystal? The CEO?" the woman said looking surprised. "Do you have an appointment?"

"We…" Lauren began.

"We don't need an appointment," Robert

interrupted, smiling at the woman. "We're family."

"Family?" The receptionist raised a hand to her mouth, covering the 'O' of surprise it made. "Do forgive me. I wasn't aware that Ms. Crystal had more children."

"You must be new," Robert said, then added, "and you're forgiven."

Eva and Lauren stared at him as if he had grown an extra head.

"Of course, you're here to visit your sister too…" the woman nodded, speaking almost more to herself than the visitors.

"Our sister?" Lauren said.

Eva elbowed his. "Of course," she said. "Our sister."

"Dear, dear sister," Lauren stalled.

"Very dear," Eva said. The children looked at each other awkwardly.

"The stories we could tell you!" Robert

slapped his knee a little too loudly, and fell quiet again.

"Well then!" the receptionist said brightly, breaking the uncomfortable silence. "I'll just buzz you in. I'm sure you know the way." She smiled.

"Of course we do. *Duh.* err... thank you," Robert nodded.

The befuddled secretary swiped her access card which opened the massive ice door leading to the office, and watched until it swung shut behind the waving children. Then she went back to waiting pleasantly for the next visitors.

"Robert! It's scary how easily a fib rolls off your tongue!" Lauren scolded as they made their way deeper into the building. "What's going to happen to that woman when her boss finds out she let strangers in?"

"She'd never have let us in without some kind of appointment. Trust me – that was the only way to get into this building and save

Christmas. You should be thanking me once again for my quick thinking."

"I suppose," Lauren sighed.

"I don't usually lie," Robert assured them.

"Unless you're trying to avoid being eaten by troll in Leprechaun Land or something," Eva said giving Robert a shove.

Robert grinned. "Again – you're welcome. Now, let's walk toward the middle of the building. That's usually where the elevators are."

If the friends had any concerns about looking like they knew where they were going, it wouldn't have mattered. The employees were more concerned with the business of making winter weather than they were with three children. Each of them had his head deeply buried in a report, or was briskly striding somewhere looking frazzled, so the unexpected appearance of the strangers didn't even make a blip on their radar.

"Hey, the elevators," Eva pointed.

"Riiiight," Robert said loudly, strolling to the elevators and looking around. "I can't wait to see *mom* again. How 'bout you guys?" he yelled as he winked at them over and over.

"Oh, stop it, Robert," Lauren whispered, pushing the elevator button. "You're not fooling anyone."

"I'm *undercover*, Lauren," Robert enunciated as the elevator announced its arrival with a jingle like a sleigh bell. "Don't blow it for me."

"Uh, what kid says he can't wait to see his mom again?" Eva shook her head at him.

Robert thumbed his nose at the girls as the door opened, and people exited, rushing to their meetings or glancing at their watches.

"What floor?" Eva asked.

"The important people in my Dad's office, always sit at the top," Robert replied. "Hit ten."

They huddled together listening to the soft sounds of 'Winter Wonderland' piped into the elevator and watched the buttons light up until they reached the top floor.

With another jingle, the doors opened to the reception area. From the ceiling hung *real* snowflakes, the floor was gleaming white marble, and more ice sculptures embellished the already-elaborate suite. The children hung back until Robert had to hold the door open or they'd have missed their stop.

"May I help you?" a man asked them from behind a delicate silver and ice desk.

"Ummm…" Eva took a deep breath and stepped into the room with Robert and Lauren following. "We, um…"

"Oh yes, you're here to see Ms. Crystal. The receptionist downstairs let me know you were coming." The man smirked at them and raised an eyebrow. "I'm sure Ms. Crystal will be very eager to meet her other 'children.'" He used his fingers to make air quotes and let them know that he wasn't fooled by their little fib.

"So, should we go straight in?" Robert asked.

The assistant gave them all a smug smile and replied, "How about you have a seat? I'll let you meet the Ice Queen – if that's what you really want." His expression implied he wouldn't recommend it.

The girls ushered Robert to the white sofas and sat down trying to look as if they really belonged there.

"Pssst!" Eva hissed out of the corner of her mouth. "Look!" She rolled her eyes toward a corner of the room, and when the children followed her gaze, they saw a door labeled 'Roof.'

"Dragon!" Lauren mouthed.

But no one knew how to sneak from the couch to the door without the stern secretary stopping them. Before they could make a plan, the unexpected shrill of a woman's voice from behind the closed office doors caught their attention.

"Motherrr! Why do you have me selling ice

cubes to the locals? No one here wants to buy ice! You are wasting my talents! *Wasting* them! I should be Vice President in charge of Northern Light Magic! *You* of all people know how I've *toiled* over baby teeth and Golden Dust. Surely you can't just disregard all of that experience! Ice cubes – indeed!" The children's mouths hung open. It sounded as if a foot stomped from behind the door, and they knew exactly whose foot it was.

"Well, Dearest, you know the company expects background checks..." Another voice said more quietly. "And until you provide me with references, I am powerless to advance you."

"References?!" the first woman shrieked. The children heard loud stomps punctuating her response. "I'm!" (stomp) "Your!" (stomp) "DAUGHTER!" (STOMP!)

The assistant looked at the children unfazed. "Diva is a little high strung," he smirked. "But you already know that. She's your *sister*, after all."

"I was afraid of that..." Robert gulped. They stood up to make a hasty exit when the door to the fancy office flung open and out stormed their familiar foe.

With her customary extravagant white ball gown flouncing behind her and her white hair piled high upon her head, she was gritting her teeth and stomping her way toward the elevator when she saw them and stopped dead in her tracks.

"So you've decided to heed the note I left! Still hoping to save Christmas?" Her sharp nails stabbed in their direction and her nostrils flared. Slowly an evil smile crept across her face as the children cowered before her in silence. "Welcome to Mumsy's Winter Weather Corporation. You're just in time! I've been considering a career change and I could use some baby teeth Magic."

14. A Sparkling Personality

The children shivered and held hands for courage, while the assistant openly gaped. "Mumsy? Then you really are related? And you came here *anyway*?"

Diva whipped her head around and glared at him. "I heard that," she hissed. "And how dare you insult me. Get out!"

The man's eyes grew large. "What?"

"You heard me!" Diva shouted. "You're fired! Now get out!"

"But... but... why?" the man implored.

Sensing an opportunity to distract her, Eva said, "He *did* say you were 'high strung.'" She smiled at him and shrugged.

"Yup, I heard that," Robert nodded.

Now the assistant had Diva's full wrath, but as she narrowed her eyes and opened her mouth to unleash another, even more brutal tirade, a woman appeared in the doorway.

"What in Winter's Name is going on here?" The woman was much shorter than Diva, and had a few more wrinkles, she was dressed in an fancy silver business suit and had the same white hair as Diva. The children could clearly see this was Ms. Crystal, the CEO. *This* was Mumsy - Diva's mother.

"Ohhh!" Eva whisper-shouted. "Go, go, go!" She pushed Robert and Lauren toward the door to the roof, lugging their backpacks with her. The children broke into a sprint around the reception desk, dodging Diva who had jumped into their path in an attempt to catch them. As she spun around grabbing for Robert, she ran into the stunned assistant. "Get out of my way!" Diva yelled, "The little brats are not getting away from me this time!" But she couldn't keep up with the children's

frenzied spins and dodges as they ran from her grasping hands.

The children rushed to the roof door and gave it a shove, and since Diva kept tripping on her dress, she didn't stand a chance of reaching them. Instead, she stomped her foot (again) and wailed like a child, "Mother! Don't let them get away! They are horrible children and they'll ruin everything... I need those baby teeth!"

"Again with the baby teeth, Diva? That's so beneath us!" Ms. Crystal sighed.

Then the heavy door slammed shut behind them and all they could hear was Diva's muffled whines growing fainter as they raced up the winding stairwell toward the roof.

At the top, was another door labeled "roof". This one appeared to be made of steel. "Okay," Lauren panted, mopping the sweat from her face daintily. "What's the plan?"

The plan, Eva thought. The plan was to burst onto the roof and jump the dragon, terrifying it with the element of surprise, until it surrendered the Northern Lights and whimpered in submission. The three of them would work together in unison, needing only their Junior Detective instincts and finely-tuned karate skills to startle the beast. Their unparalleled non-verbal cues and mastery of every tool in their backpacks would return the Lights to the skies, repair the TimeBender and save Christmas, earning them Santa's special favor and a permanent plaque at the North Pole. The local paper would herald the children as heroes and Eva would never have to clean her room again.

"Motherrr! Hurry!" the piercing voice ricocheted up the steps as Diva opened the door below.

"The plan is to *hide!*" Eva shouted. The children heaved the second door open and burst onto the roof with a crash.

Even so, this did not disturb the dragon on the roof top, which merely snuffled and snorted as it shifted around.

"Robert, Lauren, look in your packs. Did my mom leave us anything to block this door?" Eva asked spinning around and looking for something to help.

They both shook off their packs and dug through them in a frenzy. "Heeeey!" Robert shouted almost immediately. "There's a chain and a lock in here. Where did this come from? It wasn't here before. I'm telling you, I would have known. I mean, feel this thing! It's *heavy*. How…"

"Just chain the door!" Lauren shouted.

"Oh, right."

Eva held her back against the door while Lauren wrapped the chain around the handle. Robert snapped the heavy padlock shut and said, "That should give us a little time." The children slumped against the door when they heard a growl behind them.

Slowly they turned around, they were now just feet away from the thief they were here to capture. "Ohhh, myyy…" Lauren was visibly shaking.

The dragon groaned and ignored them as it rubbed its swollen belly.

Eva pressed her back more firmly against the door and blinked hard at the glistening blue and green dragon. It was the most beautiful creature she'd ever seen and she was afraid she might cry. Its massive bat-like wings were neatly folded down its back, and it seemed to be very uncomfortable.

"Wow," Robert whispered.

None of them could decide whether to be terrified by the sheer size of the beast or hypnotized by its colorful splendor. But they didn't have time to find out, because they heard the shrieks of one furious Diva and her CEO mother pounding on the locked door. Eva gasped and waved her hands frantically to signal that the friends needed to hide – and fast! – when suddenly the dragon rolled over, exposing a belly swirling with all the colors of the Aurora Borealis.

"Ohhh," Lauren whispered, "Look! The dragon is a girl! She looks like her tummy's upsetting her."

The three were mesmerized again. Lauren was right. The dragon's swollen belly was glowing; the colors swirling around like a gas cloud. Her front legs cradled her belly and she snorted softly. Her long lashes fringed tear-filled eyes.

"Uh, guys?" Now Robert heard the sharp 'ping' of the metal chain being broken, and pointed to the door. "We need to hide."

The friends looked around desperately. The roof was flat and exposed except for one gigantic dragon and a couple of small vents. "Over there!" Eva whispered.

The children sprinted on tiptoes to the short wall behind the dragon, equally afraid of the beast and getting caught by Diva and her mother.

"I bet the pretty dragon doesn't want to be stealing Magic for this Snow Corporation!"

Lauren huffed in a whisper, "I bet they're making her do it. We have to help her!"

With a crash, the lock broke completely and the door flew open. "Penelope!" shouted Ms. Crystal. "Move, you stupid dragon!" If the children had any confusion about where Diva got her sparkling personality, they were crystal clear now.

They ducked behind the wall just as the dragon jerked and moaned, rolling over again on its belly. When she raised her head the children could see the round, older woman shaking some kind of stick at the creature. She stood very tall on her knobby, stick legs, and her curly white hair would have reminded them of Mrs. Claus, except for the grim expression on her face. Penelope cringed away from whatever Ms. Crystal was shaking.

"Penelope! There are children somewhere on this roof top," the woman commanded. "Find them for me..." The stick glinted in the moonlight, and the children could see it was an icicle wand. "Then... *eat them*."

The children gasped and shrunk back down.

"Uhhh... Robert? Do we have anything else in the pack that can help us now?" Eva's voice warbled. "I'm sure my Mom thought of everything."

"I'm checking... I'm checking." Robert rummaged through each of the pockets.

The dragon sniffed the air and turned to face the children directly behind her. Her large head lowered and her orange eyes quickly focused on the three children pressed up again the stone wall in a huddle.

"Ah! There you are," Ms. Crystal screeched. "I see you've met my new pet. Isn't she a beauty? Nursed back to health from a nasty little run-in with some dreadful snow creature, and *such* a help now! Why, the sheer volume of Magic this beast can inhale is simply astounding. Who knew?" She gestured toward Diva who was now standing behind her short, round mother looking huffy with her arms crossed over her chest. "My daughter has told me all about you trouble-makers. You'll see that I take care of trouble-makers quickly. Especially those that interfere with the family business." Her laughter had the same tinny quality as her daughter's, and the children knew they were in deep dragon doo doo.

"I could have handled this, *mother*, if you'd have let me take the wand!" Diva pouted.

"Quiet, dear. Let mother take care of this," Ms. Crystal gave her daughter a stern look. "Now, you know how unbearable Diva is, but you haven't yet seen the likes of me!"

"*Thank* you, mother," Diva smiled smugly. "Wait, what did you say?"

"You may think your family has the market cornered on Magic, my dear," Ms. Crystal continued, her eyes flashing at Eva, "but I assure you, that is not so. You'll soon see that when Magic is involved, *we* are just as good as the snotty O'Hare family."

Diva simpered as Eva grabbed her friends' hands. "Yes!" she sneered, "and if Santa thinks he can carry on without the Magic of the Northern Lights, he'll be sadly disappointed!" She stomped her foot. "It's just not fair! Why do children like *him* better? How come no one ever wrote *me* a letter or left *me* cookies? I brought children *money*, for cryin' out loud!"

Ms. Crystal rolled her eyes. "Diva, dear. This isn't the time. Santa needs Magic and he needs snow. We happen to be in control of both, so just calm down. Now, Penelope!" she commanded again with a twirl of her wand. "I *said*, eat the children!"

A grey mist began to flow from the wand, spreading around the dragon's head. Penelope careened back and forth as the fog covered her, and she moaned, clutching her light-filled belly. Diva clapped with glee as the evil little CEO continued to command the fog onto the dragon's head, forcing the dragon to turn and slowly open her jaws toward the cowering children.

"Eeek!" Lauren squeaked. "Somebody do

something!"

"Yes!" Diva shrieked with laughter. "Somebody dooo something!" She threw her hands in the air, mimicking Lauren's distress.

The dragon's eyes were fixed on the children in a dull stare. She was close enough that Eva could see her reflection in its huge eyes. "Wait... A reflection! Reflections do the opposite!" she thought, remembering the small mirror her mother had given her. The question was – where was it?

Eva wracked her brain. Where was that mirror?

The dragon's breath was warm in their faces. Drops of drool hung like ropes from her mouth, her sharp teeth glistening in the moonlight. "Nice Penelope..." Lauren whispered. "Niiice Penelope... Who's a good girl? You're a good wittle girl. Schmoopy woopy. Yes you are! Yes you are!"

"It won't work, silly girl," Ms. Crystal sneered. "She doesn't even hear you right now."

Eva's hands searched frantically, and finally she grasped the fancy mirror tucked safely deep down in her pocket.

Ms. Crystal laughed sinisterly, and shook the wand at the dragon. "Penelopeee," she said sweetly. "Eat! That! Child!"

Eva jumped up, pulling out the mirror and opening it as she raced toward Diva and Ms. Crystal.

"Eva!" Lauren cried.

The dragon swung her head around to snatch at Eva but before she could close her jagged teeth on the girl, Eva leapt into the air with the mirror held high and aimed it directly at the stream of fog coming from the wand. When the fog touched the mirror it reflected the grey Magic, bouncing directly onto the CEO of Snow.

The dragon closed her mouth with a snap and shook her head. She looked as if she was

waking from a dream. Robert sat down with a thud and Lauren buried her face in his shoulder. "I can't look," she said.

The wand's fog had now completely engulfed Ms. Crystal's head, and she turned to her daughter with a strange expression on her face. When she opened her mouth, the children were sure she was going to shout at Penelope again, but instead she turned and bit Diva on the arm.

"OWWW!" Diva cried. "Motherrr! You bit me!" She pulled her arm away. "What are you doing?" Diva's panicked voice screeched as her mother moved toward her hungrily.

"I must eat a child," her mother said in a flat voice. Her eyes were glazed and her teeth were bared.

"No! Stop it! Give me that wand!" Diva commanded, backing away quickly.

"Eat! Child!" the CEO shouted.

"I told you those children were trouble!! Give MEEE the wand!" Diva shouted, sprinting toward the stairwell.

It was the last thing the children heard from her as Ms. Crystal raced down the stairs after her child, the magic trailing behind them in a thick cloud.

15. If We Can Just Get her to Burp...

Robert let out a whoop and pumped his fist into the air. "Yeah! Eat *that* child!" he shouted. The dragon studied Robert with bright orange eyes. "Get it? Because Diva is Ms. Crystal's child?" Eva could have sworn the dragon was having a good laugh, too, from the look in her eyes.

"Yay Eva!" Lauren yelled jumping up and down and clapping her hands.

Eva cautiously side-stepped the dragon, who didn't seem to mind the children at all now that the fog had lifted. Penelope simply tilted her head like a puppy as she watched them, patting her glowing belly.

"Hey look," Eva said. "I don't think she wants to eat us after all."

"Are you a good wittle girl?" Robert baby-talked to the dragon.

"At least he didn't say 'we come in peace,'" Lauren snarked. Even Robert couldn't help laughing now.

"Poor thing," Eva said, becoming serious again as she watched Penelope. "She looks so uncomfortable." Indeed, the dragon's head had drooped, and she continued to rub her stomach as if to calm the jumble of colors inside her.

"I wish we could help," Lauren said. Suddenly the dragon let out the tiniest burp, and a wisp of shimmering light escaped and floated back into the air. This seemed to make the dragon feel a bit better.

"You guys!" Lauren pointed. "Did you see that? We can get the Magic back up into the sky at the North Pole if we can just get her to burp."

"Now *that* is my kind of Magic!" Robert said.

The children stared into the sky as the light evaporated.

"Well that's no good," Eva said, peering up at the stars. "One burp will never be enough."

"We need that wand," Robert said.

"And just *how* do you propose we get it?" Lauren wrung her hands together.

The children were stumped. Penelope buried her head under her tail and groaned. They watched as her distended stomach roiled and bubbled with the trapped magic.

"Wait a minute!" Robert said, jumping into the air. "I've got it!" He reached into his backpack and produced the golden Coin Eva's mother had given him.

"Oh! Yes! I forgot about that! I bet this is the Coin my mother won in Leprechaun Land!"

"So *that's* why she put it in the pack for us," Robert said. "I'll never doubt her again," he added solemnly.

"Go ahead, Robert," Lauren said. "Make a wish."

"Okay. I know *exactly* what to wish for but we need to get Penelope away from here first." He moved toward the dragon, motioning for the others to join him. Gingerly, his hand ventured forward to rest on her heaving side. "Isn't she beautiful..." he marveled.

"We really should hurry, Robert," Lauren worried, "Diva and the Ice Queen could be back at any time if Diva manages to get that wand away from her mom."

Robert nodded. "Hey," he crooned to her, "do you think you could help get us all off this roof top?"

Penelope leaned her long neck down and lowered her body so the children could climb up, then she stretched out her leg and nudged Robert closer.

"I think she knows we want to ride her," Lauren said in amazement. She rubbed the dragon's nose softly, as if it were a reindeer, and Penelope made warm, rumbling snorts.

She was still a dragon, however, so the snort covered Lauren in green goo from the knees down. "Ugh...gross." Lauren backed away covering her mouth.

"Cool!" Robert laughed, patting the dragon's side. "I'd give *anything* to take her home! You think my mom would let me keep her?"

"Don't be ridiculous!" Eva replied matter-of-factly. "Dragons are not for keeps. We're only borrowing a ride, so don't you *dare* use that Coin to wish you could keep her!" She turned and began the careful climb onto the Penelope's back.

Lauren watched Eva's ascent, her mouth wide. Then she looked at her snotty feet. And *then* she looked at Penelope's grimacing face. "Yeah, Robert. Didn't you see how unhappy she was being controlled by Ms. Snow?"

"But... But... I would *love* her." Robert turned to pat the dragon again. (Penelope seemed to at least partially understand the conversation, and her eyes suggested that she thought the idea of having a little boy as a pet was funny.) The dragon gave Robert another nudge with her nose, pushing him toward her back. He sighed and climbed up to sit behind Eva, but Lauren didn't budge.

"Okay, upsy daisy now," Eva said patting the empty spot on Penelope's back.

"Oh, I don't know..." Lauren hesitated. "She looks awfully, uh... *slithery*... And, well, I think maybe Robert should just wish us all to Santa's Workshop so we don't have to... uh... fuss with the whole dragon riding thing."

"Yes, that's a good idea," Eva agreed. "Get on with it, Robert. Let's just use the Coin now."

"Oh no!" Robert crossed his arms and scowled. "I am not going to come *this* far and *not* ride a dragon!"

The children heard a clattering of footsteps from the stairwell again, and the muffled shouts of, "Motherrr! Give it to me right this instant!"

"Robert! Come on!" Lauren stomped her foot.

"Nuh uh! No way!" He closed his eyes and held his backpack tighter.

Quite suddenly, the door to the roof slammed opened and interrupted the children's argument. Diva came charging toward them, tripping on her hem and mopping the sweat from her forehead. Ms. Crystal charged along behind her on stumpy legs, trotting as fast as she could.

"Give me that compact!" Diva shrieked. Her glittering heels kept catching in her long gown, and if Ms. Crystal's legs were even an inch longer, the ex-Tooth Fairy would have surely been gobbled up by now. The CEO never stopped chanting, "I must eat a child," as she tried to catch up with her daughter.

"Fine, Robert, you win!" Lauren cried, leaping for the dragon and shutting her eyes tightly as she slid onto the shimmering, scaly back. Penelope opened her opalescent blue and green wings, unfolding them with a loud 'snap,' and knocking over Diva and her mother, who bounced on their behinds with Oofs and Uggs while the children clung to the dragon's neck.

Penelope looked back one more time at the children balanced on her back. Her eyes were dark and as shiny as a wet stone. Her wings created a mighty current in the night air, and the children leaned forward to hold on tighter as she bounded upward and began to soar.

"Whooopeee!" Robert shouted, almost forgetting to hold on.

Eva leaned in close and shouted to Penelope, "Can you take us to Santa's Workshop? He needs us there. All of us!"

Penelope's only response was a loud hiccup, but she flapped her wings harder and they soared even faster.

The ride was surprisingly smooth once they were high enough to glide. As far as the eye could see, the ground was blanketed in sparkling snow, and the moon felt close enough to touch.

"Look!" Eva shouted above the wind. "There's where we snowboarded! I wonder if we can see the Abominable Snowman!"

Robert craned his neck around the dragon's giant head trying to spot the beast. "Nope!" he shouted, "but there's the trail!"

The children cheered, partly relieved that the monster was behind them, partly energized by the exhilarating ride, and partly giddy that they were going to save Christmas after all and their adventure was nearing the end.

Or so they thought.

16. Hang On!

The children laughed out loud. Lauren had even forgotten about the dragon snot all over her legs and had raised her arms in the air with the others – pretending they were flying all by themselves.

"This may be our best adventure yet!" Robert hooted.

"I love our adventures and all...and this is a lot of fun, but sometimes I wish we were just normal, regular old kids." Lauren sighed, pouting over the loss of her hat.

"Not me!" Eva squealed. Robert nodded giving a fist punch into the air. "Though I do wish my mom would tell us how she knows all this stuff. Hey, speaking of 'stuff' – Robert what did you do with that Golden Coin?"

"It's right he..." Robert began, when suddenly Penelope took a great dive toward the ground. Robert would have slid right off of her back if he had not managed to catch Eva's coat and steady himself.

"Why are we going down so fast?" Eva yelled over the wind.

"Look!" Lauren yelled back pointing to the earth below. "It's Santa's Workshop! It must not be that far from Snow Corporation by air."

"Aren't we coming in awfully fast?" Eva asked, holding on tighter to Lauren while Robert squeezed in against her back and clutched the Coin tightly.

The dragon turned steeply, spiraling toward the middle of the cobblestone square in the center of the city. "Robert! You better make that wish right now!" Lauren squealed.

"I'm on it!" Robert shouted gleefully. He held the Coin up between two fingers and whispered something to it. Instantly, it sparkled and cracked in two, hovering in the air for a split second before splintering into a million sparkles and fading away into the night sky. Lauren and Eva breathed a sigh of relief; the wish was made and they'd be safely on the ground in no time. Christmas would be saved. They'd each get a warm hug from Santa, cups of hot cocoa, probably a few extra presents, and be home by midnight. Eva patted Penelope's side and said, "Robert will find you a safe spot to land. Don't you worry, girl."

"Okay guys! Hang on!" he shouted, as the dragon continued her downward spiral.

They clung to Penelope as she dove, and through squinted eyes, Eva could see that Elves were beginning to scatter, dropping packages and abandoning pushcarts as the dragon loomed above them.

"Robert!" Eva shouted, she felt her stomach

lurch into her throat. All this spinning was starting to feel like an out-of-control roller coaster ride. "What did you wish for?"

But Robert had no time to answer, for just then the dragon hit the ground with all four paws running. As she galloped, the squealing friends slipped and slid forward on the great dragon's outstretched neck. At last she dug her claws in and stopped very suddenly, causing the children to roll over one another down her neck until they bumped and crashed to the ground, landing in a big heap of knees, shoulders and legs in the snow.

"Well, hello!" said a voice somewhere above Robert's knee (which was resting on Eva's ear). "They're new to dragon riding. You can always tell the new ones. They haven't got the hang of the landings yet." This was followed by lots of high-pitched laughter.

Eva pushed Robert's knee away from her ear and sat up angrily. "Robert! What was that? We could all have contusions! I thought you said you made a wish!"

"I did!" he defended himself. "Look!" He pointed to a bottle of soda the size of a school bus.

"You wished for a soft drink?" she sputtered, looking around at her surroundings, her irritation momentarily interrupted by what she saw. If she didn't know better, she would have thought she was dreaming.

Everywhere she looked was there was glittering, sparkly garland. Ornate Christmas trees of every size and shape could be seen throughout the snowy streets and, in a small pen nearby, reindeer were grazing on what looked like red licorice grass. Elves stood nearby offering the reindeer what appeared to be gummy bears as treats. It almost looked like the fence was made of - no, it couldn't be - peppermint sticks?

"Uh, hellooo?" said the Elf, tapping her clipboard. Eva slowly looked up into the nostrils of…

"LiLu!" Eva shouted. She and Lauren jumped up and rushed forward to greet their friend.

Robert remained on the ground with his mouth hanging open (Eva hoped his tongue dried up) and LiLu jingled up and down with excitement.

"I know where we are!" Lauren cried gazing around at the glorious Christmas village. Another titter of group laughter arose.

"Well, I should think so," hooted the head Elf. "Someone had to give that dragon directions." The crowd snickered again.

Robert finally spoke, "The dragon!"

In the commotion everyone had forgotten about Penelope, who had loped over to the soda and was now finishing off the last of it. She placed the empty bottle on the ground with a loud clank, causing everyone to jump. Then she sat, blinking at everyone – who sat blinking back at her. Her tail swished back and forth and she licked her lips.

"Atta girl!" Robert shouted, running toward her.

She seemed to smile at him, when a strange

look crossed her face. A loud rumble came from her tummy and the lights inside her belly began to bubble like a lava lamp.

Everyone took a step back and stared as Penelope began to throw her head back and forth. Her belly expanded until her skin looked almost translucent and everyone could see the glow of colors shining through her scales as if she had swallowed a rainbow.

Slowly she began to beat her wings against the night sky. The Golden wishing dust, which had been whisked away after Robert's wish, now fell softly like snow around her, circling her body like an ever-tightening belt.

"She's gonna blow!" Robert cried, flailing up and down and pointing.

All of the Christmas commotion stopped and Elves began to run for the toy factory. As the dragon roared, stretching her neck, everyone who was still outside either ducked behind a Christmas tree or merely hugged their neighbor in terror.

No one knew what to expect. In all the history of Christmas, this had never ever happened. Sure, there had been other crises (the coal strike of 1902 left Santa without any lumps to leave for children on the Naughty List, and the heated debate over whether to add red stripes to candy canes in 1900 almost shut the Workshop down that year). But there had never been a catastrophe of such magnitude at the North Pole.

Only Robert remained calm. "Come on, Penny! Let 'er rip!"

And then, the longest, loudest belch ever witnessed in all of history began.

Penelope gave her massive chest a hearty pound, and out rumbled the sound of a garbage disposal, which soon got louder and louder – a lawn mower, then a motor cycle, then a jet plane taking off. Robert began to laugh and jump up and down as she belched. "Do the alphabet!" he shouted. "Say the alphabet!" The Northern Lights poured out like a rolling fog, in shimmering greens and yellows, blowing the children's hats off and knocking down fences.

The children and Elves covered their ears (and their giggling mouths) and everyone relaxed a little as the burp continued past its crescendo. The roar of the jet plane turned down in notches: A garbage truck, a motor boat, and then an espresso machine. Red and blue lights swarmed around ankles and snaked up tree trunks. Finally the sound of a growling puppy, an electric razor and one final hiccup – like the pop of a gum bubble. The last bit of the Aurora Borealis puffed out, a final opal of color, from Penelope's belly.

Little heads began to peep from windows and Elves began to loosen their grip on trees and candy cane fence posts. Robert beamed, close to tears. "This is the happiest day of my life," he squeaked.

The colorful mist crawled across the ground like a rolling rainbow fog. Its beautiful colors spread out around the Christmas village, seeping into every door and window and crack, covering every inch of the town.

The dragon sighed, looking down at her belly, which was once again flat and solid. She patted it, making satisfied little rumbles and snorts, and when she looked up at the children who had released her from her imprisonment at the evil snow corporation, Robert could have sworn he saw a *'thank you'* in the dragon's eyes.

Robert raced forward to hug a giant leg, and the entire town began to cheer. "You saved Christmas, Penelope," he said. "We should be thanking you." The dragon nuzzled him and he buried his face in her neck, clinging to her.

"Come on, Robert," LiLu touched his shoulder. "We have to let her go."

But Robert just nestled closer. "I'd take care of her! I promise! I'd walk her and feed her. I'd even clean up after her!"

Eva scowled, imagining the size of the little "presents" the dragon would leave in his yard. "Robert, if you love something you have to set it free," she said.

"What does that even *mean*?" he wailed.

"Uh, I don't know," Eva stammered. "I've just heard grownups use it in situations like this."

"Oh, you mean like when some kid *really*, really wants to keep a pet dragon? You mean in situations like *that*?"

Penelope rose up now, spreading her wings gracefully.

"Where will you go?" Robert cried. "Where will you live? What if you're captured again?"

But she merely lifted gracefully into the starry sky. Taking one last glance around, she gave Robert a wink of her long lashes. Then it took only a couple of quick beats of her powerful wings to carry her off into the night.

Robert wiped his eyes. She was gone.

"Well, that went well!" Eva said turning to LiLu with a satisfied smile. "All of the Magic is back! Everything is fixed now, right?"

But a wailing, "Ohhh nooo…" was all LiLu had a chance to respond before the chaos erupted.

17. You Can't Handle the Clipboard!

The children gaped at the sudden activity. Elves in firefighter uniforms were running toward the toy factory with long licorice ropes and fans, occasionally stopping to tie something down, and then rushing back to fan the fog away.

"We have to do something!" LiLu cried. "This Magic needs to be up in the sky. It's affecting everything it touches!"

"But I thought it would float!" Eva shouted, moving out of the way of several Elves rushing by with more fans.

"Me too!" she shouted. A loud boom erupted from somewhere inside the toy factory and

LiLu spun around and began running toward it.

The children raced to follow her. When LiLu reached the sparkling double doors, she flung them open and gasped at what was happening inside. The colorful fog was causing chaos everywhere. Stuffed teddy bears were flying through the air and candy was swirling out of machines in oozing blobs. The loud speakers played "Walking in a winter... Walking in a winter... Walking in a winter..." in a loop. But worst of all was the smell of burnt cookies.

LiLu shook her head and pressed her palms against her cheeks. "Elf Number Two! Number Two?" she shouted over the skipping music.

Eva was breathless from all the comings and goings around her. She was just about to ask about 'Elf Number Two' when she felt a great pinch on her arm.

"Ouch! Robert!" she shouted, rubbing the spot.

"Sorry," he said, looking around with wide eyes. "I wanted to see if I was dreaming."

"You're supposed to pinch *yourself* when you want to know if you're dreaming," Lauren giggled at him.

Just then a red-haired Elf with the biggest ears they'd ever seen rushed up to stand in front of LiLu.

"You called, Boss?" he said.

"Yes. Mike, do you think you can handle the clipboard?" she asked with a raised eyebrow. "I have to go get Santa so we can move the Magic back into the sky. That means you'll be in charge of this zone for a while."

"Oh! Oh, yes!" The Elf beamed at LiLu. Eva noticed that his ears were now almost the same shade of red as his hair. "I graduated head of my class in Project Toy Management, you know! I won't let you down!"

"Alright, then. I'll check back with you after I've met with Santa. We've never missed a deadline, so don't make this time the first!"

Eva was impressed. LiLu may have been as pretty as a little doll, but she was one serious manager. "Now try to get this place in order while I get these kids to Santa." She handed him the clipboard.

"I won't let you down, boss!" the Elf said with a crisp salute. But just as he accepted the outstretched clipboard, a nearby machine began launching cream pies directly into his face, knocking him completely off balance. The children stifled giggles and LiLu put her head into her hands and groaned.

"It *is* strange..." LiLu mumbled as they walked past the machine tossing pies. "That machine is supposed to be making roller skates. I suppose Mike is lucky he didn't get hit by one of those."

Mike, who had ducked out of the pie slinging trajectory, shoveled cream off the clipboard, and squinted at the very soggy paperwork attached. "I *still* won't let you down, boss!" he shouted as they hurried away. "You just leave it to me! Head of the class! Head of the class,

you know!" He readjusted his hat and scurried off to disable the faulty equipment.

"Well, we'd better hurry! I can only imagine what's happening throughout the rest of the factory. Now, follow me to Santa's office. He keeps the TimeBender there under the tightest security – even I don't know the combination to the safe. I can't imagine what would happen to time if the fog got to it! I'm not sure even Eva's dad could help us!" LiLu spun around and headed through the crowd of rushing Elves dodging flying red and green goo.

Eva, Lauren and Robert had to hop to keep up with her brisk pace. (Not to mention stay out of the way of bustling Elves trying to wrangle Magical madness.) Randomly catapulting candy and toys made getting across the room a bit of an obstacle course, and if Eva and Lauren hadn't steered Robert deliberately, he would have surely been derailed by the sheer volume of candy.

"What was she saying about your Dad?"

Lauren panted as they raced after LiLu.

"I don't know either," Eva scowled, "but I plan on asking Santa when we get to his office."

Across the large room, they stopped at an arched doorway framed in gumdrops. Christmas trees shielded the entry on either side.

"This entry is our high security level and only opens with a secret code." Sneaking a look over her shoulder, LiLu touched the gumdrops in a pattern alongside the doorway: green, red, white – white, red, green. Then the door clicked open and she ushered the children into the hall beyond.

Eva thought her eyes would pop out of her head! She turned to look at Robert and Lauren, but their mouths had dropped open and neither could utter a sound.

"Whew! This room doesn't seem to be affected by the fog," LiLu sighed. "We should hurry along to Santa. Follow me, please."

The children could only stop and stare as LiLu rushed forward. Eva lifted her eyes to get a better view of the high ceiling in the circular room, but it was impossible to see it all. Shelf after shelf of dolls spiraled in stacks so high they could not see the top. A giant library of action figures, fashion dolls and rag dolls of every size and color were standing next to one another wearing every imaginable costume, seeming to rise up for eternity.

In the center of this room stood a machine run by three Elves. One was at the conveyor belt, carefully placing a bare doll on the machine's runner. The second Elf was in charge of pressing the correct buttons, which were labeled, 'Action Hero' or 'Military Fatigues' or 'Ballerina' and so on, depending on the type of doll on the conveyor belt. The doll would then emerge dressed as directed, to be meticulously inspected and placed upon the available shelf space by the third Elf.

"Ahem!" LiLu cleared her throat from across the room. The children snapped to attention. "As you can see, this is our doll production room," she shouted over the machinery. "I'll show it to you later, but now we really must go." Eva nodded, hurrying to LiLu's side, but Lauren stopped to gush over a baby doll that drank from a bottle and closed its eyes when she cradled it, and Robert lingered at the enormous doll machine, staring at the dials and knobs.

"LiLu, how does this thing dress the dolls so quickly?" he asked, leaning in farther to peer into the opening where the conveyor belt revolved.

"When everything's working properly, it dresses the dolls even more quickly…" she began, turning back in time to see the colorful fog seeping under the doors and spreading toward the doll machine.

"Robert! Don't lean in there!" LiLu cried. With a simple snap of her fingers, the other Elves in the room looked up and rushed toward him. But the fog was faster. As Robert watched doll after doll slide into the machine, the fog quietly swirled around him, lifting him into the air. It was only when he landed on the conveyor belt that he noticed at all.

"Grab his feet!" LiLu shouted to the Elves still running toward him.

But before they could unplug the doll dressing machine, Robert disappeared inside.

18. Dolly Dominoes

The fog closed around the doll machine and it began to hiccup and buck with Robert inside. The Elf workers rushed around pushing buttons and pulling levers but nothing worked.

"What do we do?" Lauren wrung her hands.

"Over here!" LiLu cried. "Hold my feet!" Santa's Head Elf pushed her hat farther onto her head and leaned over the conveyor belt. "Don't let go, whatever you do!" she warned, and reached inside as far as she could.

Lauren and Eva grabbed LiLu's feet, while the machine workers held Lauren and Eva. Robert's shrieking voice came from far inside the machine, and Eva feared this might actually be the end of him.

LiLu grunted and struggled. Ten seconds went by, twenty. One of the Elves shouted for reinforcement, and several rushed into the room, their adrenaline high from battling the fog.

"I think I've got him!" they finally heard. With one last heave, LiLu flew backward, landing on Eva and Lauren and toppling the rescue workers.

One of Robert's hiking boots dropped from her hands, but other than that, nothing remained of him.

The machine shuddered to a stop, and Lauren looked at Eva, tears in her eyes. The Elves stood in the silence, waiting for LiLu to tell them what to do next. Santa's Head Elf dropped her head. "We still have to warn Santa about the fog," she whispered finally, standing and heading toward another door.

"What about Robert?" Eva cried, pointing to the machine.

LiLu stopped and shook her head. "He's

stuck. We'll have to take the machine apart later... There's nothing more we can do now. *Now* we have to think of Christmas and all of the children!"

Poor Robert... her detective partner and dear friend... Eva sniffed, feeling horrible. If it weren't for her, they'd never be in this mess. If her mother hadn't known so much about Magical mysteries, Robert would still be at home this very minute, sound asleep, dreaming of Christmas.

Everyone jumped when the machine gave one last splutter and spewed several dolls into the air. They landed in a pile a short distance away.

"That! Was! *Awesome!*" The muffled shout came from beneath the plush mound of toys.

No one could really blame Eva or Lauren, or... well, *all* of them for their laughter. Because, Robert, had popped up from a mound of Baby Burpy dolls dressed in what appeared to be a mix of three costumes. In place of his pants, he wore a lacy princess skirt complete with frilly petticoats. His shirt and coat were now replaced with sparkling fairy wings. (Just wings. No shirt.) But in Eva's opinion, the best part of Robert's transformation was his face. Beneath a lopsided pirate's hat, his cheeks were rosy with blush, his lips were red and glossy, and his lids bore the loveliest shade of shimmering blue eye shadow.

Eva found herself belly laughing so hard she tumbled backward. Then everyone laughed – and they might have *continued* laughing except that when Eva fell, she stumbled into a shelf of dolls.

And when that first Spinning Spencer doll wobbled over, it knocked its neighbor, who knocked *its* neighbor, setting off a chain reaction (which would later be known as the Great Dolly Domino Disaster), that continued for eternity up the spiral shelves toward the ceiling that was so high it could not be seen. Eva sat on the floor with her mouth gaping, the first tipped doll lying in her lap.

"Oh, LiLu! What do we do?" Eva yelled above the sound of doll after doll tipping over.

Just then Elf Number Two rushed into the room. Mike glanced nervously from LiLu to the other Elves who were either trying to catch falling dolls or were frantically pushing buttons on the hiccupping Doll Dresser (which was now puffing rainbow sparkles from either end).

"I've got this under control!" he assured her. "The Engineering Elves are on their way. May I be so bold as to make a suggestion, boss?"

LiLu raised an eyebrow at him.

"Well, er, if you approve, that is… I'd, uh, like to suggest that you take the visitors out of the room so we can fix their mess… Uh, I mean, *organize* the zone."

LiLu smiled just the tiniest bit and then nodded seriously, dismissing her protégé, who saluted crisply and began shouting directions at eager Elves.

Lauren shook her head. "I'm guessing Mike

will be updating the manual after this one?" she said to LiLu.

"Indeed," she said, "Now we really must hurry before the fog spreads any farther!"

LiLu ushered the children from the room and once the door was closed behind them she turned and said gently, "I don't want you to worry. Santa's house is Magical and we've had emergencies before. I mean... nothing like this, of course, but everything *usually* straightens itself out by Christmas. We just need to get that Magic back into the right place!"

Eva's face burned bright red, but Robert, who was busy tripping on the hem of his skirt merely replied, "Do I have to wait until Christmas for a pair of pants?"

"Not at all," LiLu said with a flourish of her fingers. "Santa's office is right through here. I'm sure he can help you." When LiLu turned again, the children gasped to see that behind her there had appeared a door.

"It's soooo pretty!" Lauren said clasping her hands and sighing.

"Thank goodness the fog hasn't touched it!" LiLu breathed.

Eva touched the heavy wooden doorframe. How could she have missed a door like that? The wood was carved with elaborately decorated Christmas trees, and people singing carols or exchanging gifts. It was the most beautiful door Eva had ever seen.

"Wowww…" Robert whispered. "Every time you turn around, there's something new to see…"

"Don't touch anything!" Eva admonished, her face still red from the dolly disaster.

"Everyone in," LiLu shushed, gesturing for the children to enter.

The children stepped through the door, mouths open, eyes wide. Of course, the halls leading to Santa's office were as dazzling as everything else they'd seen. More Christmas trees lined their path and life-size Nutcrackers stood at attention along the walls.

"A little faster, children," LiLu prodded.

Eva shivered in anticipation, and found she was even a little bit nervous. Robert didn't appear to be nervous at all, tripping over his gown and gawking at the blown glass ornaments and garlands seemingly made of spun silver.

LiLu continued nudging them onward past all the sparkle and ornaments until finally they came to an abrupt dead end. A large plaque mounted on the wall read: "Christmas is not a time nor a season, but a state of mind. To cherish peace and goodwill, to be plenteous in mercy, is to have the real spirit of Christmas." Under the words was a hand-signed name. Eva squinted and moved closer. Calvin Coolidge! The thirtieth president of the United States! How amazing that Santa knew Mr. Coolidge! (Eva laughed and caught herself. Amazing that Mr. Coolidge knew Santa was more like it!)

"Well, here we are!" LiLu announced.

"Here where?" Robert said, beating Eva to the question. The children spun around in a complete circle to evaluate exactly where "here" was, and as they faced forward again, they saw the door.

"Well... I never!" Lauren smiled.

But enough was enough for Eva, who blurted, "First you're telling me my dad is involved in Christmas somehow, and now this! I know for a proven fact that door was not here just a second ago. It is scientifically impossible."

"Really?" Robert smirked. "A 'proven fact?' So you're a scientist now?" Eva felt her face redden again.

"Well," she stammered, "Maybe not... But I know that I didn't see a door here before!"

Lauren shook her head, "Christmas is Magical, Eva. What other kind of entrance would you expect?"

LiLu nudged them through the door, and all the talking stopped, for there, in front of them, was Santa's awesome office.

19. The True Magic of Christmas

Santa looked up from his enormous desk and gently laid down his golden quill pen. Then he took off his spectacles and smiled such a welcoming, warm hello that the children felt they'd just been hugged.

Robert, grinned back and said, "Hiya, Santa!" then broke away and ran to him, practically knocking him out of his huge stuffed chair.

Santa scooped Robert up into his arms and gave him a small toss into the air. "Well hellooo there Junior Detectives. I've been eagerly awaiting your arrival. In fact, you're just in time." Robert was so giddy, he didn't remember to ask for a pair of pants. Even Eva didn't think to ask how her father was involved with the Workshop.

Eva and Lauren raced over and waited for their hugs. Santa's white beard bounced over his full chest as he let out a deep chuckle. He put Robert down and reached forward to hug Lauren. Eva was so excited that she leaped up and down, grabbing Robert's arm and hugging it for all it was worth. Robert blushed, but he didn't stop her. How could he? With Santa, you just couldn't help but hug someone.

"I declare!" Santa boomed, reaching out to hug Eva next. "It is so good to see you again! Have you solved the case of the Christmas Crime so quickly and brought us back our Magic lights? Perhaps not quite where they belong, eh?"

Lauren nodded vigorously, looking very serious, "You know about that?"

Robert poked her in the ribs, "Of *course* he knows. He's *Santa*. Duh."

Eva bit her tongue. "What's the matter, Eva? Are you worried about getting home by midnight?" Santa asked with a sly smile.

"Well, yes... And there's the fog... And the dragon. And, well, the dolls are probably *still* falling over. And I didn't believe there was really a door, and LiLu knows my dad, and Robert fell into the machine, and then that big gigantic soda pop. Come on – a *soda*?" Eva rambled, then blushed harder and looked at her feet.

"It sounds as if we have quite a dilemma here!" said Santa, in a way that told them he didn't think it was a dilemma at all. He looked merry and playful. "What you don't realize is that your brave actions are already being paid forward. Our problems should be solved very soon, so there is no need to worry, children." He held his belly and chuckled deeply, seeing their confused expressions. "Ah! Do you understand what I mean when I say 'paid forward'?"

Eva was sure it had something to do with something they'd learned in school about banks or money, but she opened her mouth and closed it again, looking at the others. Reluctantly the children shook their heads.

How embarrassing that their motley Junior Detective crew didn't understand what Santa was talking about...

"Perhaps if I show you a little Christmas Spirit you will understand. Besides, it always gives me a lift." He helped Eva off his lap and told the children to sit on the floor. Then he looked up at the ceiling and gave a little wink. A small door opened (where there was none before!) and a shining bubble floated down to them until it was just at eye level. The children gasped and gathered in a circle around it. It looked like a glowing crystal ball!

"Look into the globe, children. Tell me what you see."

At first, Eva could only see snow swirling around in the wind, but slowly the snow dissipated and other images began to emerge. "Oh!" she exclaimed. "I see a boy helping a lady pick up the grocery bags she spilled."

Robert sat up on his knees looking into the globe. "I see a man sitting on some steps," he said. "Hey, there's that lady! She's handing the man one of her bags of food!"

Lauren leaned forward and the scene in the Magic ball changed again. "I see a dirty little puppy. Oh, he looks so cold and wet..." Lauren's eyes filled with tears. "I can't look," she said.

"Wait," Eva grabbed Lauren's hand. "Look!"

"There's the man from the steps! Oh! He's sharing some of his food with the puppy. And look, his little tail is wagging so hard he's about to knock the guy over." She giggled and wiped her eyes.

"The scenes keep changing," Eva said, looking at Santa with wondering eyes.

Even LiLu smiled happily as she watched the images inside the Magic crystal ball. "I never get tired of this," she sighed.

The children knelt closer to the Christmas globe, their hands outstretched as if it offered the warmth of a fire, captivated as the snow shifted from scene to scene of kindhearted acts. "Here's one you'll be particularly

interested in, dear boy," Santa said, patting Robert's shoulder.

Robert leaned in closer. "Hey! There's Rudolph!" he shouted. "Wait – who's he flying with?"

LiLu giggled, and Santa put his finger to his lips.

"It's Penelope!" Robert bounced up and down. "Hey girl!" he waved to the crystal ball. "That's Penelope!" he smiled at Santa. "She's my dragon!"

Just as Eva was about to tell him he certainly didn't own a dragon, Santa pointed at the globe again. "See what your dragon is doing, Robert. Watch how she's passing along the kindness you paid to her."

Penelope broke away from Rudolph and began her descent to the ground so fast she left behind a sparkling vapor trail in the night sky. Robert looked at Santa fearfully. "What's she doing?"

"Just watch, child," he nodded.

Just as she threatened to dive to her demise, Penelope spread her wings like a parachute and landed gracefully in the town square. There, she stretched to her full height and, rearing up like a powerful stallion, she began to flap her mighty wings. As the gust churned and blew, the colorful fog was sucked from every nook and cranny it had invaded until it was propelled into the sky. Penelope rose with the force of her wings, working the mighty winds to contain the Magic around the tops of the Christmas trees. She roared and her breath flared into flame. With one final powerful flap, she angled a burst of dragon breath, and the Northern Lights spiraled up into the vacuum she had created, like a colorful cyclone. Penelope flew with them into the sky, guiding the Lights until they spilled upward and settled amongst the stars, once again blanketing the earth with the intense glowing colors of the Aurora Borealis.

The children leaned forward as if in a trance and lightly placed their palms against the globe. "She did it," Robert said. "She really did it..." The swirling snow seemed to expand and surround them as the scene shifted once again. Eva giggled as she now saw Santa's Workshop. The children glimpsed the Elves using the restored Magic of Christmas to resume toy and candy production. Mike was tapping his clipboard cheerfully and the cleanup crew had swept away all the broken candy canes to be used later for spinning cotton candy. Even the doll room was completely in order.

The scene in the globe changed again and the friends smiled as they watched a father reading his young daughter to sleep; a teenager sitting with her grandmother at the beauty parlor; a man offering his seat to a lady holding her infant. The children were so caught up in the beautiful scenes of grace and love that they didn't even notice Santa's office slowly fading from view around them.

Receding into the mist, they did not see him put his hand on LiLu's shoulder or present to her the restored TimeBender. They didn't see the room glowing around them or hear the

Carol of the Bells. Not even Robert smelled the mouthwatering fragrance of freshly baked cookies.

"Grace, children," Santa's voice echoed with laughter, "this is the heart and spirit of Christmas. Grace. All else is just a parade – even Christmas ornaments fade. For it isn't the tinsel or holly, you see. It isn't the presents under the tree. It's grace and kindness – which were here from the start. The true Magic of Christmas comes from your heart."

And with the last reverberation of Santa's words, the swirling snow faded away with the joyous images they had been watching. The children found themselves back in Eva's bedroom, kneeling on her floor with each of their hands pressed flat against each other's.

20. From Your Heart

Eva blinked and looked around her room.

"That was so cool!" Robert whispered. "Did it really happen?" He looked down at the pair of snow pants he was now wearing, along with his original shirt.

Lauren laughed, "I'm pretty sure it did Robert." She turned him toward Eva's vanity mirror so he could see the doll makeup on his face.

"Awww," Robert muttered, wiping at the makeup with his shirt sleeve.

"I wasn't ready to leave!" Eva squealed. "There was so much more to see! Do you think we can go back?" She rushed to her book shelf and pulled out her favorite

185

Christmas book, which she opened to a picture of Santa's Workshop. "This isn't exactly like his *real* Workshop," she said grabbing her friends' hands and pulling them toward the book. "But on the count of three let's just jump in, okay?"

Robert nodded with a grin and held her hand tighter.

Even Lauren nodded eagerly, when a concerned look crossed her face. "Wait, don't we have to make a door?" she asked.

"I think we just need to believe," Eva assured her friends.

"Ready?" Everyone held their breath. "One! Two! Three!" They all jumped up...

...And six feet landed straight on top of the picture. The spine of the book made a little snapping sound as they continued to stand there.

"What happened?" Robert asked Lauren. "Is each picture good for one ride? Or do reindeer have to come pick us up?" Lauren simply shrugged.

"Don't you remember what Santa said when you were looking into the globe?" a voice asked from the doorway.

"Mom!" Eva cried and raced to hug her mother.

Mrs. O'Hare laughed, planting a loud kiss on the top of Eva's head. "I'm so proud of all of you. You must have had such an adventure!" She looked at her watch. "And it isn't even midnight yet. Now *that* was some excellent teamwork!"

"Not even midnight! The TimeBender *is* real!" Robert shouted.

"It was so exciting!" Lauren grinned and hopped onto Eva's bed.

"I want to go back! I'm pretty sure they needed me to help in the Workshop," Robert pouted and prodded the book with her toe. "And hey, how did you know what Santa said to us?"

Mrs. O'Hare smiled and sat down on the bed next to Lauren. "It's what he's always said: 'The true Magic of Christmas comes from your heart.' Perhaps you need to find the Magic of Christmas for yourselves."

"But how? We don't have a Magical globe," Eva said. Then she looked at her mom closely, "Do we?"

"All the scenes we saw were people helping others," Lauren whispered. "Caring for others... Sharing..."

"Oh! Now I get it," Eva smiled. "I know someone I want show I care. You, mom. I never realized how much you share the Christmas spirit with me every day."

"Thank you, sweetie. I'll always cherish those words." Mrs. O'Hare put her arm around Eva's shoulder and stood up. "How about I bring you children a late night snack? You must be starving after your snowy adventure!"

"Yes, please!" Robert crowed.

"Great! When you've had your snack you can come downstairs and get your overnight bags. Lauren and Robert, it's a sleepover at our house! I told your mothers earlier today that you'd be staying here tonight."

"Earlier? Like, before Diva showed up in my room?" But Eva's mother only winked.

The three children grinned at one another. None of them were ready for the adventure to end and they would probably be up all night talking about it.

"Hey mom, can you knock when you come back with the snack?" Eva asked.

"Whatever for?" Mrs. O'Hare laughed and shut the door behind her.

With her mother safely down the hall, Eva rushed to her bedroom closet and opened it up to rummage around. "I'm going to make mom a little box that she can keep her special things in," she said.

"What're you going to make for your dad?" Robert asked.

"Hmmm... I think I'll make him a calendar. He's always looking at one," she said.

"That's a wonderful idea!" Lauren agreed enthusiastically. "I'm going to make my grandmother a book that she can put all her pie recipes in."

"Mmm... Pie..." Robert said absently. "Hey, Eva, can I use some of your supplies too?"

Eva nodded and brought out a tote full of colorful construction paper, pens, glue, scissors and stickers. "Who are you making a present for?" she asked.

"Lauren," he said, blushing just the slightest bit.

"Me?" she asked. "What for?"

"I saw you hugging that doll when we were back in the Dolly Division. I know mine'll only be a drawing, but it was a nice doll..." He blushed harder. "I mean – for a *doll*."

"I'll hang it in my room, and it'll always remind me of tonight," she smiled at him.

The children worked diligently, cutting and coloring and pasting their special projects. When they were done they sat back to admire the gifts they'd made. Lauren marveled at Eva's paper box, Eva complimented Robert's baby doll drawing and Robert helped Lauren put the finishing touches on her grandmother's recipe book by including an index entry for "Robert's Favorites."

The children were interrupted by a knock at the door. "Eva, can you help me?" Mrs. O'Hare's voice said from out in the hall. Eva opened the door to find her mother balancing a tray with cookies and cocoa. "Oh, Robert – grab that for me, will you?" she said as the plate began to slide.

The children each took something to lighten the load, and before Mrs. O'Hare turned to leave, Eva said, "Mom, come look at what we made!"

"Are you sure?" she laughed. "It isn't even Christmas yet."

"I just can't wait!" she bounced up and down.

"It's a box! It's a box!"

"It's a lovely box, sweetie," she said turning it around to examine it from all sides. "And look, there's even a little handle for me to open it with. How very clever of you."

"It's only paper," Eva said.

"You made it with love," Mrs. O'Hare said gently. "And it's perfect."

"It would have been more perfecter if it was carved out of wood," Eva said.

"Well, hmmm..." her mother said. "It looks like wood to me."

And there, in front of them, the paper box Eva had so lovingly created grew heavy in her mother's hand. It started from the bottom, where Eva had colored birds and flowers. Charming carvings of sparrows and tulips seemed to spring to life as the paper disappeared and rich, glossy wood took its place.

The children's mouths hung open. "I don't

know why this should surprise me..." Robert gasped, turning to find the gift he'd made for Lauren. He held the drawing out toward her, and as she took it from his hands, a small baby doll materialized, gently closing its eyes as she nestled it in her arms.

"Hey, quick! Someone draw me a picture of Penelope!" he said.

"Oh, Robert..." Mrs. O'Hare sat on the bed and frowned. Robert sulked over to grab a cookie.

Eva sat on her mom's lap. Her eyes were very heavy from their busy night. "How do you know all these things, mama?" she asked, settling into the crook of her arm.

"You know I told you that someday we'll discuss how I know what I know. But for tonight..." she looked at her watch again. "Goodness! It's late, and I know a few certain someone's that need to get some sleep."

"But I'm not even tired," Robert said yawning.

"Of course not," Mrs. O'Hare smiled. Eva had crawled down from her mother's lap and the children were lying on the floor with their art supplies spread out around them. Their eyes were heavy and they all looked ready to fall asleep at any moment. Mrs. O'Hare glided around them picking up the art supplies and removing snow shoes and jackets. Then she cuddled each one up with warm blankets and pillows from the bed. "Listen, children. When I was a little girl, I went to Santa's Workshop."

"Now we're getting somewhere!" Eva yawned, rubbing her tired eyes.

"I've learned a lot of lessons over the years, but this one I'll never forget: Magic – *true* Magic – happens when it comes from the heart. You can take it with you to any land, whether there are Fairies or Leprechauns, Elves or dragons." She brushed Robert's hair out of his eyes. "And the best Magic is used with love."

"Uh huh," Robert said nodding into his

pillow.

"In fact, the Magic from your heart is a big part of just about every celebration. Remind me to tell you about the Magic of Valentine's Day some time."

Lauren mumbled her agreement, half asleep already.

"Go to sleep now, children. It's the morning of Christmas Eve and Santa will be expecting his cookies tonight." Mrs. O'Hare lingered a moment, giving her daughter one final caress. Then she blew them a kiss from the doorway, turned out the light and shut the door.

And, strewn about the floor like crumpled wrapping paper, the children were all fast asleep before the Golden sparkles from her kiss had even faded away.

The End

Here ends The Case of the Christmas Crime. Stay tuned for our detectives next adventure when a little Valentine mischief tangles them in a love spell in, The Case of Cupid's Con.

Please visit us at our website, www.magicalmysteryseries.com to find other magical adventures and learn more about the authors and illustrator.

Made in the USA
San Bernardino, CA
08 February 2015